# DURABLE TUMBLERS

# Durable Tumblers

*by*

## Michael Kenyon

*Michael Kenyon*
*Oct. 97*

oolichan books
Lantzville, British Columbia, Canada
1996

**Canadian Cataloguing in Publication Data**

Kenyon, Michael, 1953-
Durable tumblers

ISBN 0-88982-157-7

I. Title.
PS8571.E67D87 1996          C813'.54          C96-910445-6
PR9199.3.K423D87 1996

The author gratefully acknowledges the following publications:

*The Malahat Review* for first publishing "Durable Tumblers," *Prism International* for "The Angels in Cities" and "Chaste," *Epoch* for "Salvage," *NeWest Review* for "Chinese Ideas," *Event* for "The Day it Snowed on Maurice," and *The Fiddlehead* for "Crèche." "Chaste" also appeared in Oberon's *Best Canadian Stories*. "Durable Tumblers," shortlisted for the National and Western Magazine Awards and the Journey Prize, also appeared in *The Journey Prize Anthology*.

The author also wishes to thank the British Columbia Ministry of Tourism, Small Business and Culture for financial support during the writing of this book.

Oolichan Books acknowledges the support received for its publishing program from the Canada Council's Block Grants program.

The publisher and author are grateful to Sarah Gee for permission to use a detail from her work "Abduction & Annunciation II: Incident at Dallas Road" as the cover image.

Published by
Oolichan Books
P.O. Box 10, Lantzville, B.C.
Canada V0R 2H0

Printed in Canada by
Hignell Printing Limited
Winnipeg, Manitoba

# Contents

# Durable Tumblers

*I can't remember the first part*
*of the only song I knew by heart*

—Sam Gentles

In the autumn of the year I turned sixteen my father taught my sister and me to drive, and my mother planted one hundred tulips.

That prairie winter was the longest, coldest, whitest I can remember, so we had zero opportunity for street practice and had to settle for sitting behind the wheel of Dad's Ford while it was parked—still warm from his long drive home from work—in the two-car garage.

As the ice fell in chunks from the underside of the vehicle onto the smooth concrete floor, forming rivulets of water that meandered back toward the double doors behind which the latest storm raged, and as we waited for our father, who frequently would not return to give us our lesson, Moira and I found ourselves talking about deserts. My interest was poetic because that winter I had had my first shivery brush with sex;

Moira's fascination was with geology and time. A year older than I, but to my mind incredibly naive, she grew obsessed that winter with how earth would look at the end of its life. We sat in the garage till our teeth chattered.

In the spring, while I grew proficient at double parking and somersaulting into the back seat, Moira gave up driving and decided to become a desertologist. Most of Mother's bulbs were successful. She had great plans for her small yard. Every evening after dark, while Father filled out job applications, she sat beside him at the kitchen table with pencil, graph paper, catalogues, and she plotted beds, rockeries, rose arbours and trellises. In nearby chairs, Moira consumed large books whose covers bore images of golden dunes, and I waited for the phone to ring and longed for my legs to turn that colour. In the summer Father got the position in Vancouver, and he and I drove the family out of our lovely crescent, our narrow suburb, out of the prairies and over the Rockies, till we were in a moist, spectacular and jarring world that would no longer support our safe, familiar sense of family.

I'm twenty-eight now. I've been trying to have a baby for the past twelve months. Before that I was on the pill for eleven years. My period's a week late, and I just spoke by phone to my husband who called from work to see how I was, did I feel any stirring, any prescient nudges? A routine call, but one that leaves me, soon as I've hung up, with the sense that I've not said enough. The middle of the day, when he's gone, has become a wasteland. The doctoral thesis I'm supposed to be writing exists only as a bunch of notes, a reading list, and a gnawing guilt aligned somehow with my, ahem, unfruitful loins.

I'm thinking this as a hundred papery Holland bulbs surround me on the living room carpet. Geoff and I were to go to Hawaii for Christmas, to relax and listen to our bodies, but have had to change our plans. This change has created another desert beyond the bounds of the daily one—a much larger barren place that recently boasted an ocean, a hotel room, soft intimate music. We must go away now in November, not to Hawaii, but inland to spend time with Geoff's mother in southern Alberta and with Moira in Calgary. Geoff's mom has had a small stroke, and my sister has completed another series of electric shocks—her second or third, I can't keep track. We leave tomorrow to drive a loop and do what we can; assess each situation, says Geoff.

He's forty-eight, Geoff is. Nearly six-and-a-half feet tall, big-boned and fleshy, he jogs to keep at bay his father's paunch. He has flat feet, a Roman nose too high on his face, and thinner and thinner sandy-brown hair. He's an accountant with a brokerage firm. He's simple in a good way, meaning uncomplicated, though he has occasional amazing flashes of insight. His parents emigrated from Manchester when he was fourteen to homestead just east of the foothills. He scored the only goal of the first soccer game he played in Canada, got his name in the town paper. Tonight he will watch something called Crystal Palace vs Man United. He's written it on the calendar. With the sound low, he'll lean close to the TV, whispering "yes!" and groaning. He watches the same games over and over. All he will say is that the games make him feel sad, as though he's failed in some way, but also warm and nostalgic.

I should go out in the rain and dig, but I feel weird. It's as though I'm homesick, sick for a home that does not yet and might never exist, sick for another place, another me. I don't seem able any more to deal with Geoff's straightforward vision of the world, his resolute desire for children. I don't seem able to make time for anything. I can't even find a moment to tell him how a baby might overpopulate me, might use up all my oxygen.

Some of the bulbs are soft, they should have been planted a month ago. My parents are dead and I've dealt with that. It's been raining since September, and the dirt is sopping wet. I panic at the prospect of seeing Moira, yet I no longer wish death on her husband, who has trusted doctors and signed papers. The middle of November is so dark.

"Our son, if we have a boy, will probably never be a football player," Geoff says.

"No," I say, ignoring his wistful tone. "Probably never."

"Those guys are so young, Pam," he says. "I mean, when I played, when I was a kid, they seemed old."

"Golly," I say, "Geoff discovers the march of time."

"Well, something happened to me when I stopped playing, when I stopped going to matches. Things started moving, and I mean too fast. The professionals're twenty-five to thirty years younger than I am now." Awe in his voice.

"So?"

He turns to look at me, large soft hands spread, wanting me to understand. "They're so serious," he explains. "They hug and kiss one another when they score a goal."

He is a funny, dear man, and I am so bleak. I hug him. He hugs back. I hold him at arm's length and, laughing, tell him how his "Man United" gives me the heebie-jeebies. I tell him I've started my period. I do not say how well "Crystal Palace" describes the hard, cold, fragile structure that fills my head these days.

"It's all right me watching the game, then?" he says. "You don't despise me for it, sweety? I had the feeling you thought it was stupid."

"Go ahead," I say. "It's fine."

Before going to sleep I lie on my back and listen to Englishmen roaring at Wembley. Roaring and singing. "Auld Lang Syne" and "You'll Never Walk Alone." I think about my sister, in and out of the hospital, how I'm helpless because she lives so far away and trusts her husband and he's satisfied with her course of treatment and she won't or can't go against his advice. He's always been jealous of our relationship, hers and mine, and won't listen to my suggestions of alternate therapy, new doctors. He's not an evil man, I tell myself. He visits her for hours every day she's in hospital. He looks after their two kids when she's gone, shelters them from her extravagant ecstasies when she's home. He's stolen her from me and his goal is her death or her permanent incarceration. And damn him, he'll shoulder his eventual freedom and guilt with a martyr's good grace.

My own husband sits in the dark, rewinding, reviewing each goal, the feints, tackles, dives, exultations of each player. We're safe here, under our roof.

When the game finishes, he comes to bed. "Great to see a good goal scored," he says, climbing in. "You asleep?"

"Why?" I mumble.

"I never wanted to give up playing. I just didn't get along with the others. I couldn't get into the drinking and chasing chicks and toughing it out with the other goalscorers. I only loved my life out there between kickoff and the last whistle. Time expands when you're in the middle of a game. Everything's clear and simple. But so little of the whole business of soccer takes place on the field."

Now he tries to interest me in making babies. My mind spins out across some bare cracked landscape in a dream of flying, wanting to stretch our round tense limbs till they're as thin and relaxed as telephone lines. And he's on the green field, no doubt, counting defenders, assessing paths of interception, his eyes on the goalie, gently pounding his way toward the netless posts. Or maybe he's thinking of the phantom baby, or of another woman. It galls me that no thing can be itself, that sex can't be just sex, love love, pain pain, longing longing, Geoff Geoff, Pam Pam. The dirt out there in our yard is heavy clay, nothing like the dusty topsoil my mother used to try to anchor against the wind, nothing like the thin dirt Geoff and his father worked on their big poor farm. Just now, as we both drift loose, I imagine being a cypress. Moira told me once that desert cypresses are the oldest trees in the world, that some have lived four thousand years. I plant myself in this clay, sink roots to some impossibly deep and distant water, stretch my leaves in arid air, and wait, and slowly grow, while all about dwindles to desert. Eventually, perhaps, I'll want my branches full of agile new creatures.

As usual when we travel together, I do all the driving so Geoff can stretch out his long legs, and we listen to the taped books I picked up at the library; when our ears are tired, we talk about sex.

"My parents stopped after I was born," says Geoff, yawning. "Dad died in '82. That means he went without for forty years. Unless he was unfaithful."

"What a word!" I say. "Without faith, faithless, untrue. You don't really believe he was celibate?"

"No question. I can't imagine him with another woman. Mum told me they stopped when I was born."

"Did you ask her why?"

"She told me fat people didn't need sex as much as thin people."

"Oh sure. Was it mutual?"

"I don't know. I assume it was his decision. She's a strong-minded woman, but I mean if he'd wanted to, then they would've. When we get there, let's put it to her."

"Moira's even thinner than I am and she has no interest in sex."

"No? So you think maybe lack of physical love could be responsible for her present situation?" His voice grows soft, as it does when he's on uncertain ground, and this annoys me nearly as much as the content of his words.

"Physical love? What the hell is that?"

"Well," Geoff says, "we need it, you and I." Then, attempting humour, "You yourself," he says, "are pretty good evidence for the thin argument, Pamela."

"Oh yes?" Christ. Gentle Jesus save me from idiocy.

"Oh yes!"

In the first motel room we have a long bath. We drink Irish whiskey. Geoff massages my stiff neck and shoulders. We make love: we eat each other up. Lying on my belly on the bed I reach down to the carpet to twirl one of the empty glasses. These drinking glasses, made in Japan, are called Durable Tumblers. In the night there's a blizzard. I wake several times to great gusts of snow blowing against the window. I dream that I am Japanese. I'm standing barefoot on some old worn wooden stairs inside a room whose walls and high ceilings are of deep polished red wood. Light floods the house, comes from windows concealed behind screens. My hair is loose, longer and blacker than it really is. The man I've been expecting enters the room beneath me. A diminutive American gangster type with shoulder pads, he walks slowly toward the stairs and begins to ascend. When he's on the step above the one on which I'm standing his eyes are level with mine. For a moment I believe he will continue up. But no. Without looking at me, he bends a little, reaches down into my kimono and grasps between my legs, his finger skilled as a hummingbird beak. I quickly avert my eyes, breathe in. We remain, joined, for a long time. Then he cups his free hand round my nape. My hair hangs heavy over our points of contact: the last strands follow the tense veins of his lowered forearm. We are to kiss.

"Maybe this trip will be as successful as Hawaii," says Geoff.

"Huh?"

"Maybe more successful," he says.

"More successful?"

"Didn't you feel something last night, Pamela?" he says. "Something different?"

The rest of the morning I drive without speaking. Geoff tries a few more inane remarks, on the weather, last night's sleep, but soon gives up. He's as anxious as I am about the visit, not knowing what to expect. Iris is eighty-five, overweight, and on various medications for arthritis, high blood pressure, water retention, and now a blood thinner to prevent another stroke. And bleak and drawn, beyond the image of Iris, waits the figure of my sister, nervous as smoke, immured in some institution, all familiar gestures expunged. Already my neck is tight again, my fingers ache from grasping the wheel. Yesterday we talked of everything except what I wanted to discuss: the baby, the non-baby. Now there's only that left to talk about, and since I can't think of how to explain my change of heart, we both put on headphones and listen to the last chapter of *The Time Machine*.

"'So I travelled, stopping ever and again, in great strides of a thousand years or more, drawn on by the mystery of the earth's fate, watching with a strange fascination the sun grow larger and duller in the westward sky, and the life of the old earth ebb away.'"

The Time Traveller has left behind the beautiful Eloi of the upper world, his child lover, Weena, and the dreadful Morlocks of the lower world who kept the Eloi as cattle, and now, inspired by curiosity, is running his machine further and further into the future.

In Fernie it begins to snow, then to blizzard, and I have to slow the car almost to a standstill. I glance at Geoff. We're hunched forward in our seats, plugged in to Herbert George Wells, walled in by snow, watching the world end. I wonder if it's like this for Moira, strapped to a machine, ebbing away, for thousands of years. And do those words *strange fascination* have anything to do with Iris's condition? Geoff and I do not talk of his mother dying, yet she is dying, her body giving up, no matter how hard her mind strives to keep it going. It seems unlikely that she'll recover from this last bout. But what is recovery? Covering oneself over, putting on a mask, burying oneself? No, of course not. One recovers one's health, one's good health, whatever that is. And what is death?

"'From the edge of the sea came a ripple and whisper. Beyond these lifeless sounds the world was silent. Silent? It would be hard to convey the stillness of it.'"

Suddenly, we're in Alberta, out of the blizzard. The Time Traveller has completely vanished. Geoff decides he wants to see the farm his parents bought when they arrived here in the fifties. We remove our headphones and he directs me along the highway to Vulcan.

At Nobleford we turn west again toward a place called Granum. Dark clouds fill the windshield; the road goes straight into the clouds; thin snow blows across the blacktop immediately ahead. Several miles later, at a sign that says Trout Lake, Geoff says: "Turn right, go four miles north, then at the first intersection, turn left." Now we're on the gravel surface of a seldom-travelled concession road. Somewhere to either side must be farmhouses, mothers, fathers, children, I hope, cosy inside. This is what I want to believe, that the apparently empty and brutal world holds some pockets of warmth. But my mind tends to evil: what's the worst thing I could imagine? Death? We see three hawks huddled on fence posts. The sky seems intent on crushing. The wind buffets our little beetling car. From every direction night seems to be closing, though it's only two in the afternoon. "Hutterite colony's over there," says Geoff. "Can you see it?" I shake my head. I can't see a thing. "One mile west," he says, "at the first corner turn right, a mile north we'll see the Griffith farmhouse, a two-storey job. We turn left." He has to shout over the noise of the car and still I'm not sure I've heard him right. I lean toward him and ask did he say a mile west? When I turn to watch his lips, his eyes open very wide, something in the car explodes. Perhaps it is outside the car, but now we're sideways, going into the snow fence, upside down. My head bounces off the steering wheel and then all is quiet and I'm lying on the soft velour roof; the plastic cover over the interior light presses my mouth open.

"What're you thinking about?" says Geoff. "You're not going to sleep are you?"

"I'm imagining us in a car crash," I say. "God, it's dark and nasty out there. Maybe boredom is something we should learn to listen to."

"It's gone!" Geoff yelps.

At the same time we hit a deep pothole in the road—thump! thump!—and we're in a large clearing, what used to be a farmyard, in front of the foundation stones of Geoff's parents' homestead. All that remains standing is the row of bare trees along the old driveway and a ramshackle barn north of the house site. I turn off the motor. The wind moans terribly.

"I can't believe it," Geoff whispers. "I can't believe it's not there anymore." He hits his forehead with the heel of his hand. "There's nothing left."

He gets out of the car and I watch him kick through the rubble, then head toward the barn. Snow swirls like dust about him; he and the barn and the trees are beginning to fade. He looks small and defeated, with his round shoulders, lowered head, hands in pockets. His sandy hair is feeble and brittle and crazy as an old nest. He thinks that he can cheat death by having children! I look at my bony knees, my poor white shins between the narrow jean legs and the thick wool socks. I feel such pity for both of us. Miles from anywhere in our stupid little car.

I roll down the window. "Hey! It's freezing out there! Come back and get your toque and gloves!"

He looks up, surprised. Hesitates at the barn entrance. "Just a minute!" He leans against the bleached wood, puts his head inside. Then takes a step forward and vanishes.

"Five-thirty, capoten. Seven-thirty, sulcrate. Eight, edecrin and slow FE and vitamin E and benemid with breakfast. Ten, entrophen. Eleven-thirty, sulcrate. Vitamin E with lunch. Two, capoten. Five-thirty, sulcrate. Supper at six with surgam, slow FE, benemid and coumadin. Sulcrate and capoten at bedtime."

Geoff's mom speaks slowly and repeats, "Slow fee."

Her feet are swollen and black where she dropped the walker on them.

"That cherry pie for dessert tonight," she says, "it wasn't bad. The food here can be all right. Listen, isn't this silly?" Her smile is crooked. The right side of her mouth stays sullen. We sat with her when she ate; crumbs and jelly pushed out and oozed down her chin. Now it's evening and she's reading the newspaper to us while we perch on the edge of her bed. "'A member of Australia's Parliament was hustled off the floor for fowl play. Bruce Goodluck, famous for making bird noises during debates, was ejected by the Speaker after he dressed up as a chicken.'"

The room is tidy and institutional, every surface hard and spotless. As we've done every evening for the past three days, we'll stay with her for an hour, till her night medications arrive, then we'll leave and she will go to sleep.

"'You can be fired for casting a "lecherous look" at a co-worker under a proposed new law in Derby, England,'" she reads. "'"It's going to be difficult to define," City Council member Margaret Geraghty told reporters. "But some men are very offensive, trying to undress you with their eyes."'"

While I try to imagine asking her why she and her husband stopped having sex, or what she allows herself to imagine about death, she tells us that somebody found a man's watch on the golf course, somebody else lost an engagement ring, that someone wants to sell a green parrot—loves women and children—for nine hundred and fifty dollars.

"My!" she says.

Geoff looks at me. I look away.

"What's it like out?" she asks.

When we're with Iris, we are so married, Geoff and I. We are so cheerfully stunned that as the days go by I forget the desert, I forget terror, boredom, forget what I wanted to work out, till it's small fuzz, a dust bunny on the floor of my conscience. Iris takes what we give, and gladly, but pays no attention. She's wrapped up in herself, in herself, I think, not in dying. Entirely preoccupied with her body, its medications, its survival. She thinks of us as extensions of herself, as unreliable prosthetic limbs, or as prophylactics—living charms against the final misfortune. All our words, all our needs seem scant to her; they are scant.

Before bed, Geoff extolls the virtue of cinnamon toast. I tell him I need him to touch me, now and then, whenever he thinks of it, not with anything in mind, just a little touch of his fingers on my face, the top of my head, my shoulder, only those places, nowhere else. Every time he opens his mouth, he says fried chicken, or he says roast lamb. He's always hungry, and me, I'm constantly tired. Iris has had a stroke. She's out of hospital and into this place they call a home. Her real home—bigger in her mind than the largest institution—awaits her return. Geoff and I stay in the visitors' wing for five days. We sleep like sisters together. We don't make love. Through the paper-thin walls we hear everything, every cough. The other guests seem sicker and older than those they've come to see. Iris wants Geoff to stay till she's well enough to resume a normal life in her own house. She instructs him to arrange home care for her, meals on wheels, a wheelchair ramp, grab bars, bathing aids. I think it's fair to say we're not bad people, but we make her cry when we talk about putting her house on the market. It's clear that she won't be able to live there again, won't be able to live alone. One morning, after a bout of tears, we look at old snapshots.

"Geoff," says Iris, "the flowers should be in fresh water. I keep telling the nurse. There's the farmhouse."

"Tell Pam why you and Dad slept in separate beds."

"These were all taken one labour day weekend, when Father was younger than you are now. What a fine strong man—he looks nattier than you do, dear. Pam, you must get Geoff to buy permapress. If you stayed longer we'd have time to go through the catalogues."

"I have to visit my sister in hospital," I say.

Iris shakes her head. "Your father always dressed neat. When he got old he snored. He never once had an illness, yet I with all my aches and pains have outlived him."

"D'you want to play cards, Iris? These photos are making you sad."

"You told me you and Dad stopped having sex after I was born, Mum. D'you remember telling me that?"

"No, no. We should have a chinook by tomorrow. That weatherman with the bad squint has been looking at me funny. It's still the best station, though. Industrial espionage is on the rise. I saw a program."

"Who is this pale thin guy standing beside Geoff?" I ask.

"Yes, who is that, Mum?"

"Him? Just a farmhand someone brought to the picnic. He seemed quite sickly. I can't remember his name. He had nobody else in all the world. I expect he died a long time ago."

"Was Dad a poor lover?"

"Geoff! Honestly. Nothing wrong with my memory!"

"We've been trying to have children," I say.

"Things were different in those days. We had our son. Oh, my pills! Water, Pam, please. Perhaps we should have some cards. My mouth feels funny. My tongue. It's nice to see you two here. Soon you'll go and I'll be alone, like the man in the picture."

The evening before we leave, Iris turns wild eyes on me and asks will I brush out her hair. Geoff and I have just wished her good night and are about to step into the corridor. She stands leaning on her walker at the window of her little room as the moon is setting and calls me back.

Geoff touches my shoulder and goes downstairs.

"So you went to see the old homestead?" she says, her voice breaking. She's said the same thing at least once every day, but now it sounds like a different question. "I don't suppose I'll ever set eyes on that land again."

Next morning the three of us sit in the entrance hall of the home and I keep casting Geoff our hurry-up look, but he shows no sign of making his farewell. "I'll get the car," I say.

"I'm Thursday," is the last thing Iris says to us. She flaps a colour-coded schedule at Geoff's chest. "Before you go you must put out the garbage," she says. "I'm orange, it's November, so I'm Thursday."

"Orange, November, Thursday," Geoff repeats. "Got it."

A billboard on the highway contains the words OPPORTU-NITY PROBLEMS MONEY.

We've only just left, but I don't want to drive straight to Calgary in our present shaky condition. In less than two hours we'd be at another institution meeting Moira and Alex. We need an interval, some kind of intermission.

I can't look at Geoff because I know he's crying. I slow the car and park in a lot at the edge of the coulees and we get out and stroll down to the river, so conscious of the necessary span between us, both aware of the impossibility of touching, at least for the moment.

Walking the coulees along the river toward us is a woman and several men. I imagine lines joining all of us, avenues of power, connectedness. The chinook wind blows hard and dry and warm. We're out for a walk while a dark curve fills the November sky. My thoughts are aimless; talk has contracted to breathing. My back aches; I can hardly bend my arms.

Last night when Iris got me to brush her hair, she lowered herself to sit on the edge of the bed and miscalculated. She slid with a small shriek to the floor. No matter how I struggled I couldn't lift her more than a few inches. She kept bleating that she could not bend her legs, I was hurting her toe, it always took two men to lift her; and I got so mad as I shoved against her big soft back and pulled at her hopeless arms. Sudden sweat, everything white as I held her, counting seconds, just clear of the grey industrial carpet. "If wishes were horses then beggars could ride," she moaned. As she hit the ground again, we both whimpered and then began to giggle.

Just now I'm the woman on the trail leading along the river to the fort. I am strong and wise with the wisdom and strength of youth. The men are all strangers. I want to refuse to see the difference between them and me. I want to raise up fat women. I want to cross every border, to walk through Japan into Canada. I want states to overlap. I don't want to see what my sister has become.

I want to make love work.

Every time I open my head, I think chicken, scaredy-cat.

When Geoff disappeared into the barn something inside me exploded, but silently. Only now the deafening sound escapes into the air and fills my ears.

And my ears are still ringing when I sit with my sister in the bright modern atrium of the hospital. Her hair, once rich and heavy, is flyaway, without substance. She sits across from me, unmoving, diminished, all her life in her huge dark eyes, like a terrified and pious mouse. She's altogether dry. Her fingers feel minutely burred. Her lips are cracked.

"Oh my poor love! Your skin, it's like parchment!"

"I keep putting on lotion," she says.

The little laugh is familiar, but also diminished. I expect, indeed want her to give way to tears, but she is worse than I imagined, and she is my sister, still and undeniably. I'm not let off the hook that easily.

I dig out lip balm from the bag of groceries I've brought, watch her dab it on her mouth.

We begin by talking of her children, but this feels like necessary business. Then awkwardly we remember our own childhood. We remember that winter spent in the front seat of Dad's car, how we talked then. How we talked! And how she hated Vancouver when the family moved, how happy she was to return to Calgary, how upset we all were, especially Dad, when she gave up university after a couple of years for her oilfield job—but that worked out, didn't it, because it earned her time and money to fund all her desert trips. But of course I am doing the talking. "Those excursions!" I say. "Those wonderful photographs!" I exclaim. "All your research—you must get back to your book. Now Jackie and Dmitri are older, won't you have more time?"

"I don't have anything to show for those trips," she says. "Nothing. I was a sham. I burned everything. I was a tourist. I know that now. What's important, what is important is staying here till I'm well. I'm weak, not like you. For you things are easy. Things come easy to you. I don't mean children, they're not important. Your degrees. Yes, look at me like that, everyone does, but listen, Pam—no don't listen, I'm too pathetic to be allowed to even think of Dimi and Jack. Of course they are important. But not in a way that concerns me. They will be all right. They're healthy animals. Like Alex. Have you seen Alex?"

I say that I have, yes, briefly. "What are those balloons on the ceiling?"

She tells me there will be a celebration in two days. The opening of a new wing. All the staff, and the patients not confined, are invited. Her lips curve with pleasure. She and Alex will dance together. "That night," she says, "you must see him properly, you must talk to him. He respects you, he'll listen. Get him alone and tell him I'm going to be fine. See him by yourself, he doesn't like Geoff. Tell him I'm strong, no, not strong, strong enough. Tell him I love our children. Tell him I do love our children. Find out if he's planning to leave me. Ah, God, Pam, sometimes I'm convinced he's about to leave me. I would die without him. I'm nothing, I've done nothing, I have only him. I know it's terrible to speak this way. The shock was the right thing to do. Before, I wanted to die. Wanted the end. I feel better now. I'm a bit off today, actually. Actually I'm fine. But without Alex, I would, I'm sure, I would die. Pam, promise you'll talk to him?"

"I promise," I say. "And I'll meet with your doctor. Moira, this treatment, you mustn't agree to it again. It's wrong. I know it's wrong for you. We must find some other way."

But whatever has animated her has passed. She shows no interest in anything else I have to say. After a few minutes of trying to explain that I can't seem to get pregnant, that I'm not certain I want to have a child, that I need someone to talk to about this, I give up. I tell her I'll see her tomorrow. She throws her head back, as if to control a nosebleed.

Next day in the afternoon I sit with her for three hours and she doesn't speak a word. Once, for a long penetrating minute, we look at each other. I can see my sister deep in there: afraid, angry, confused, resentful, most of all damaged. But these are my easy words. I expect a movement in her face, a frown, a bit of a scowl—my own face practices these expressions—but she remains masked.

In the evening I'm back again, though earlier I swore I'd stay away till tomorrow. And she talks. Such long curved sentences and packed, jarring phrases that I can't catch every word, and her meanings completely elude me. Lies, half-truths. Slow and melancholy, then rapid as a machine gun. I'm not sure how much she believes or even understands what she's saying. So many crazy things—about our past, about the hospital—that at last I think I can respond, I think I can question her. But she begins to scream when I ask about her children and her relationship with Alex. I can't get her to stop. She howls. A sound unlike any I have heard. With words buried inside. Words I can't, then don't want to make out. The walls ring. The nurse arrives with medication.

I sleep a bad night, waking several times to Geoff's snoring. Now I'm exhausted. We receive permission to take Moira out and she agrees to go. She even agrees to tolerate Geoff. We drive her to this downtown fast food bar round the corner from the hospital. She says she's hungry. The controlled bounce, flash, and thrust of the place send me into a sweat, though she and Geoff look smug and slow as TV pandas. "You're so good looking," Moira says to Geoff. She laughs. "No, no. I mean all of you." She waves a hand, as if casting a spell over the whole restaurant. "You are all so good looking!"

"You're pretty all right, yourself." Geoff beams.

She smiles at him, brilliantly.

"You look much better today," I say.

The smile continues. "Afterward," she says, "we will go shopping, the three of us. I want to buy a dress, Pamela. A beautiful beautiful dress for the opening. I want you to choose it."

While we eat, she chatters about her doctors, which ones have helped her and which have made her feel bad. "It's their job, though," she says. "I don't mind them."

"I guess they're doing their best," Geoff agrees. "They're doing what they can."

"Yes!" says Moira. "That's it exactly."

She eats a massive meal. Geoff and I hardly touch our food. She tells us she's going to get her life back on track. She's going to write a book about deserts. She finishes what's left on our plates. "Just one thing," she says, looking at Geoff. "You guys have to do me a favour."

"Name it, Moira," says Geoff.

"Okay," she says. "Geoff, you have to dance with me tonight. And Moira, while your husband and I are dancing, have a word with Alex, tell him how well I'm doing, tell him I'll be home very soon. You know what to say."

As we're paying our bill at the front, she points through the glass door to an adjoining room and starts to giggle. "Look!" she says. There, framed in the doorway, in the middle of a dark closed area beside a row of trolleys used for clearing tables, is a girl of about fifteen or sixteen. She has her arms round a boy her own age and he has his arms round her and they are kissing slowly, his tongue in her mouth, hers in his. He's a little shorter than she is. His hands play up and down her sides. She reaches under his white apron, grasps him hard and moves her hand. He holds her tighter, puts his face in her hair, and flips his pelvis at hers.

"Like animals," whispers Moira, her hands joined together as if in prayer.

"Untroubled by the world," says Geoff. "Kids making kids."

We walk outside into the freezing air. The chinook is finished. I carry the image of the cold bones of her clasped hands which gave no response when I slipped my own over them.

Mostly I'm angry. Furious at Geoff. I'm wearing the wrong clothes for this sudden chill, and I left my sunglasses in the car, but I refuse to care. I don't want to go shopping. I decide we shall walk back to the hospital. The city strikes me as astonishingly ugly. Sunny highrises, and dirty snow refreezing in the gutters. Women in furs and danceskin legs marching, and bulky men looking at their reflections in the myriad plate-glass windows. No help. And I must talk, really talk, and be nice to Alex. I feel myself snarling at any man I catch giving Moira or me the once-over; but the snarl must arrive at its destination utterly distorted, because more often than not these men make a second and more detailed appraisal. We pass a gigantic parrot on the roof of a hideous and shiny restaurant full of potted plants. Loves women and children, I think. "Loves women and children," I say aloud.

"What's that?" says Geoff.

"Nothing."

"Come on," he says. "We'll freeze to death at this pace."

He takes Moira's right arm and my left and propels us along the sidewalk. The blue sky slams down on the sleek painted feathers. I can't feel the fingers in my coat pockets, can't feel my toes. How can Geoff not understand what is so clear to me? That it's wrong to bring children into a world like this one, and selfish and wrong to purposely and consciously create a child by means of a culturally co-opted biological function. By means of an act which churns the depths of our cluttered and soiled psyches. That gives patriarchal history a dutiful salute. By this time I'm crying rainbows, deep and silent. Or else the parrot's colours have rubbed off. Maybe accidental conception is all right? Maybe pregnancy would be all right if there were such things as God and faith? Maybe it's all right for the young. Maybe the doctors are wrong and I can't have babies. And maybe I won't ever get out from under the eye of that gaudy parrot. I'll freeze to death right here and now, on the edge of my husband who eclipses my sister. Oh, shit, maybe it's all all right anyway. I'm not dying yet, am I, I'm not crazy yet?

And now I open my head to see what's left. When Geoff disappeared into the barn he became a boy again, dreaming his chores, shooting that summer goal for the home team. The ghost-house assembled itself against the whirling snow. I'm shaking now, under the parrot's eye, as I shook then, sitting behind the wheel of the car. The storm-locked car. I could smell the apprehension of the new English couple. All those years ago they fluttered within the faint summer rooms. I could taste their love of the boy. A sharp bell rang from the barn and the house pulsed and something in my head broke open.

What if I got out of the car and crossed quiet snow and entered the house by the front door? In the east bedroom upstairs close the door, lie down on the bed. The single window has bars across it. A little daylight comes in and no colour through glass warped and grimy. Soft walls spotted with crayon marks. I cannot free myself, cannot move. I hear only my own breath and heart, see only the room, the subtle changes in greyness, and imagine a slight dust haze. Someone will come. I'm helpless and clean and healthy, and I wait because I'm free to wait. In his blind passion he'll set me free. I turn my head, spin my wrists, open and close my eyes, adjust my heart by breathing. It will be no curious child exploring the ruined farmhouse. I hope he will know what information to extract and how to demand it in plain language. I can't imagine what I possess that others might want. He will eventually arrive, certainly, and anything I plan to say to gain my freedom will be as vain as these thoughts which go round and round and will continue till we get back in the car and resume our journey. And it comes to me that I understand very well what's expected. To save myself I must name what I value most. If the man on receipt of the perfect answer to his first question puts away his doubts and fears, it will mean he's understood what I value, and understood that I have compromised my soul. What do I and the man share? What do we value most? A sense of home, a precise notion of borders and possessions? Home complicated by ideas of freedom? What else? I'm completely alone, as I've always been. He will come alone. How far can the family extend?

Can a person place herself within the political? What I and the man have in common is simple.

Moira swings us into a drug store beside the hospital. She asks Geoff for money and he peels several twenties from his wallet. It seems we can refuse her nothing. I'm stupified by her glittering eyes. Geoff carries the things she selects. The checkout boy flirts with her. She buys three postcards for us to send to friends at home; she buys a set of picture hangers, a TV remote control, a pack of glittery elastics and a tiny gold charm. She buys lip balm for me, to replace the one I gave her. (Anaemia, Cot Deaths, Aliens with AIDS, I read on the tabloid covers.)

"By the way," says Geoff, at our evening meal, "did you get those bulbs planted?"

I look round at the crowded restaurant, this one in the hotel where Geoff and I are staying. Where we will spend one more night. I gaze at the monstrous salad on my plate. I tell him I don't think I can do anything for my sister by talking to her husband.

"But we will go tonight," he says. "We have to go to this hospital shindig and dance. You promised Moira."

"Oh my God," I say.

"No kidding," he says.

We're silent through two martinis. Outside, it has begun to snow.

He frowns at me. He groans. "Where are we, Pam? What is this place?"

I haven't a clue what to answer. "Your mother's dying," I say. "My sister's going mad. I don't think we want any kids."

"It'll be too late to plant the bulbs when we get back," he grumbles.

"Don't fret," I say. "They're in the ground. Did you hear what I said?"

He continues to pick at his food. What a sorrowful chewing clown. He hasn't once looked directly at me since we sat here, yet he scrutinizes every new customer, giving each woman and each man his wide unblinking stare as they're led to their tables. He does this now, watching a middle-aged couple cross the room, as he swallows his food and licks at his teeth. I lean over and poke my fork into his hand; it leaves four white marks and a shred of lettuce, a drop of oil. He starts back, shocked, hand high like a hurt paw. Now.

"I said did you hear what I said?"

# The Angels in Cities

Nobody has intentions, said Les.

The van fought through gusts of wind as the little family put the pass behind them and confronted open plain beyond the foothills. Les and Anne had been talking about one of their single friends, was her recent love the real thing, when Anne wondered half-joking whether the man's intentions were honourable, he being in his forties and she in her twenties.

I mean, said Les, no one knows what the hell they're doing.

Anne said, Well sure.

How can you talk about the upper hand, when no one knows what they're doing? said Les.

Anne said, That is true. But intentions are kind of plans, and a person could have a bad plan.

Nobody has intentions, said Les. Jesus.

Isn't it beautiful? said Anne. The way it opens up?

Sure can feel the wind.

Look at that sky.

Every fall for the past eight years Les and Anne had made the trip from the coast to Lethbridge to see Anne's Uncle Hugh.

29

They admired the colours of the changing leaves, the lakes and mountains. They slept in the van and cooked meals on an old Coleman in provincial picnic sites. Always when they got through the Crow's Nest Pass and saw the prairie spread before them, they were enchanted. They'd grin at each other, saying how beautiful, how lovely. This year was different, partly because of Tony dozing in the back. Everything was more intense.

Ten-month Tony, Les said.

Look, his eyes are open, Anne said. He's looking around, he's taking it all in.

Every year the sun shone for them, Indian summer, the yellow birch leaves crunched giving off a dusty warm smell, Anne tied up her hair, Les put on his oldest clothes, and they prepared Uncle Hugh's house for winter. They installed storm windows, cleaned out closets, tidied cupboards, rearranged the freezer. Spent hours in the basement trying to make sense of three decades of trash and treasure. They slept on the floor of the spare bedroom—the room Anne had shared with her cousin most summers of her childhood—because the bed was shot. And they slept deep. The altitude, the air, always some excuse over breakfast. Uncle Hugh trundling his walker, taking minutes to cross from the sink to the fridge to find freezer jam, and Anne sitting on her hands, Les counting to ten, both fighting the urge to help, letting him serve them. Sometimes he coughed and coughed and couldn't stop, and couldn't stop, then did stop. Anne cut his nails while Les serviced his old Pontiac.

Jesus, Hugh, when you gonna trade the dinosaur? Thirty-seven thousand miles and eighteen years old.

Never, said Hugh. No way. No sir. Bury me in that car, understand?

This time last year I was big as a quarter section, said Anne.

All the fields were stubble, a warm brown. Tony was singing in the back.

Gonna take you to Uncle Hugh, said Les.

Butter wouldn't melt in that pretty mouth, said Anne.

Past Pincher Creek they read a sign saying *Head-Smashed-In-Buffalo-Jump*.

As they dipped into a coulee where a farm surrounded by trees sat above the river, Les said, Gee, I could live there.

And winter? said Anne.

It's never winter here, said Les, only Indian Summer.

Let's stop at Fort Macleod, said Anne. I'd like to feed Tony before we arrive, I'll bet he needs changing.

On the coast, Anne worked at home doing the books of several small companies. Les was unemployed at the moment. His job was to cook and clean, to change Tony. I'll change the Tone, he'd say. Anne would snort from her computer keyboard. They liked where they lived. Who's worried? Les would snap when Anne said, Don't worry. When they got back he'd begin looking for work in earnest.

Over coffee at A&W in Fort Macleod, Les told Anne he loved her. Two men at the next table discussed the outrageous price of antifreeze. Les and Anne held hands. Tony slept in the crook of Les's free arm.

I suppose we're gonna try talk your uncle into a wheelchair again? he said.

I'm not going to ask him, I'm going to just get one, said Anne. Tell him we'll wheel it around empty if he won't sit in it.

That's one way, said Les. He's stubborn. He's so scared of his friends seeing him crippled. We could go someplace no one will know him. We could go to the buffalo jump, or that Writing-On-Stone place.

Anne was smiling.

Les said, What you so pleased about?

You, she said. You've forgotten to be depressed and miserable.

Les said, I'm on holiday. You wait till we get home, I'll be twice as blue. Or maybe I'll let you support me for the rest of my days. God, I feel relaxed.

Les said, So you think Molly's just an ego trip, just hormone-bait for this new guy?

31

Anne looked thoughtful. I don't trust any older man/younger woman relationship. Too much against it being equal.

Let's go, said Les.

Outside a mild wind blew, and heaven was thick with small clouds. They fueled the van, found the Graceland tape, and headed east. It was after dark when they first saw Lethbridge, a string of fairy lights fifteen miles away, purple sky in the rearview.

Folks getting together should be like us, Les said, as they entered the city. Should be same age, same weight, same colour hair and eyes. We have minor differences. I'm a bit taller, you're six months older. Lord, we're nearly the same sex—except for Tony, except for last night.

Slow down, Les. It's fifty clicks here.

I can smell the brewery, said Les.

Maybe the feedlots, said Anne.

Tell me when to turn, said Les. I still don't know my way.

Paul Simon sang, "Losing love is like a window in your heart . . . "

And as they pulled into the driveway and parked behind the rusty Parisienne, they saw Uncle Hugh peeping from the front room curtain, and Tony started to harmonize.

Perfect, said Les.

Three days passed quickly and the visit was half over. Les managed to keep his temper, he and Hugh stopped shaving, Tony was a wonderboy, good as gold. Anne sang loud and tunelessly to her numb fingers as she tossed out of the freezer anything older than ten years. The men laughed together, self-conscious when she unbuttoned her shirt to feed the child. Everyone was talking baby-talk. The coffee was instant, the bread light as down, soft as the tone. The adults ate fish from the deep freeze, fish caught by Hugh's boys when Aunt Rose was alive, when the boys still visited. Evenings they played rummy and looked at Uncle Hugh's old slides till all were yawning. Mornings they helped Uncle Hugh down to the basement and settled him in a chair beside Tony in his highchair, then dug into the mountain of black plastic bags, holding things up for judgement. Keep or discard. Tony had the last word on everything.

One warm evening, warmer still because Anne had baked apple pie, they sat in the living room after supper with the screen door open. Les wanted to see the gas fire lit so, directed by Uncle Hugh, he killed all the lights and held a match to the jets between the iron logs. Uncle Hugh sat back and told them he'd dreamed the night before of the royal family—Princess Margaret had given him a map showing all the itchy places in the world. He told them he'd read in the paper that peasant girls in China were committing suicide in groups because they wanted to come back as the angels they'd seen in cities. He told them that the average length of a marriage in British Columbia was twelve years. It got so hot in the room that Uncle Hugh turned beet red and Les and Anne were pouring sweat before they thought to turn off the gas and go to bed.

On the morning of the fourth day they rented the wheelchair.

No way, said Uncle Hugh.

I knew it, said Les. I told Anne you'd never go.

You're going, said Anne. We're all going, Tony in his stroller and you in your wheelchair. We're going to Head-Smashed-In-Buffalo-Jump.

Perfect, said Les.

That's final, said Anne.

I couldn't climb into your van, I'd need a crane, said Hugh.

We'll use your car, said Anne.

I'll take my camera, said Hugh.


The Pontiac sounded like it had a hole in the muffler. Uncle Hugh sat beside Les in the front seat, Anne and Tony in the back. First Les took a tour through town, past the new hospital, the new mall, along Scenic Drive past the cemetery.

It's sure changed, said Hugh. Very nice, very nice.

That's where Mrs Olbrynski lives, said Hugh. Her husband shot himself in the garage, now she's all alone.

There's the building where Rose worked. Her boss just won some kind of citizen's award.

Then they roared west toward the Rockies, pushing wind. It was a grey blustery day. Coming out of the river valley they saw four coyotes.

An hour later the prairie wrinkled to make the Porcupine Hills. Dust billowed from dump trucks where work crews were widening the road to the Head-Smashed-In interpretation centre.

More like a bunker in the war, said Hugh.

Inside they looked up and saw three real buffalo on a cliff about to leap down on them, tongues lolling, eyes crazy. Indians ran the place, the gift shop, cafeteria, projection room. Indians conducted guided tours. A shy smiling woman gave them a key to the special elevator, told them to start at the top, work their way down.

What are they all giggling about? Hugh whispered.

Happy, I guess, said Les.

Makes me nervous, said Hugh.

Anne and Les left Uncle Hugh and baby Tony by a window on the top floor and ran the outside trail to the lookout. The wind blew fiercely. They couldn't hear their voices. They could hardly breathe. They stared at each other and saw teeth. Around them stretched land, trees in the river valley, water spraying off a lake by a farm. They kissed beside the telescope and sprinted back to the building, flapping their arms.

Side by side in their chairs, Uncle Hugh was telling Tony how the herds of buffalo grazed this area. Tony was examining Uncle Hugh's big rough thumb, turning it this way and that in his hands. On the lower floors were legends, artifacts, a simulated dig showing bones, and a movie. The film showed how the Indians fooled the buffalo and made them stampede by wearing calf skins and coyote skins. Once a brave hid under the cliff and watched the buffalo like a waterfall falling. He was killed, buried because there were so many that autumn.

Let's take a picture, said Hugh. The three of you, over there by the tipi. Get rid of the stroller. Kneel down, the little guy between you. Les, you need a shave. Don't fold your arms, Anne, don't look so serious.

The day before they left, Les and Anne carried all the garbage bags they'd filled with junk and old frozen food to the alley. Les took the Pontiac in to get the muffler fixed. That afternoon Anne and Les had a big fight about money. Hugh had given Les two hundred dollars to pay for their trip, and Les had accepted it. Les said to Anne that it made Hugh happy to give them money, that sometimes accepting money as a gift was the right thing to do. Anne wanted him to give the money back. He said it was too late now.

That night he walked into town and got drunk. He stayed till the bars closed and the streets were empty, the sky huge and black all round. He followed alleys to where the lights ended and looked west and saw nothing. Stars above. Ahead nothing. On the edge here, everything seemed very confusing, very fragile, but precious, precious. He thought how one day Hugh would die. He thought of the buffalo and the Indians. Out there in the middle of China families were nailing daughters' bodies to their coffins to keep the souls from escaping. He thought of his son, and of the average length of a marriage in B.C. He thought of the three of them by the tipi in Hugh's photo. The Prospector, the Businesswoman, and the Dwarf, Hugh had dubbed them, they looked so peculiar. Wind caught the prairie grass at his feet, blew him round till he faced east and was headed into town. He felt tall and strange, and didn't want to return to the coast.

He was on his way back to Hugh's, feeling sorry for himself, ashamed of not phoning Anne, wondering how to get into the house without waking everyone, when he saw the man break the window.

This small new Japanese car pulled up to the curb; a young guy jumped out with a two-by-four and smashed the window of a wedding dress shop. He poked at the jagged bits remaining, then stepped into the display and grabbed a mannequin. In a matter of seconds he was in his car again with the figure beside him.

Les couldn't believe it. This was simple, a simple act, it cut through. He wanted to laugh, it was very funny, all of a sudden he felt good. The stiff bride in the passenger seat of a Japanese car, her veil still in place, the man speeding away looking so professional.

Les took a deep breath and continued. He decided to sleep in the van.

Tomorrow he'd tell Uncle Hugh and Anne the story. It would be his return ticket. He and Anne always needed something to laugh about the day they left, something to ease the goodbyes. Once on the highway he'd tell her he planned to send Uncle Hugh's money back. They'd stop at Ainsworth, at the hotsprings. The year before last they'd stayed there and they'd made love twice.

# Frightened

*by the author and his wife*, he reads. *By sudden exposure to light.*
He stands naked in front of the open magazine and looks down
at krill.

A glossy shoal as big as a continent on the coffee table.

Fleeing.

He turns the pages and reads about a town swallowed by
earth. A story of dark matter, ghosts, things yet to happen,
people never born, some mention of a favourite who refuses
to exist. Himself. He's the one really scared. But no. If he was
that afraid he wouldn't be here. He can feel himself trembling.
He's gulping a glass of water in a motel room and it's night. It's
all right that he can't sleep. He's drinking water, turning away
from the lake too dark to see.

Flipping through the magazine, he uses the words to soothe
himself. He recoils at the dizzying orbits of hunters and hunted
and looks instead at pictures of places where he isn't. Picks up
a brochure and reads about the hot springs, where he is, where
they are supposed to be. A place discovered by Indians in the
early nineteenth century and named by whites in the eighteen
nineties. An earlier town of three thousand burned. He has

waded through the horseshoe cave of steaming water not a few times till there's a blurring of episodes.

Whether or not that's reality.

She and he.

It's a big problem.

Caused by other problems, mind you, and in turn causing the springs to stream hot underground over mineral-marbled rock. Now the charred ruins and Indians are gone, undressed locals, conventioneers and tourists fin around the warm pool, creep through the cave, then coldplunge their bodies back to their own warmth. Every trip a wakening of something that needs to be sung.

∞

After jagged sleep, a new day of driving over new mountains was ending.

They yawned through failing light, towns unpaved, unlit, mere rush of dark rooves and gas stations serving bitter coffee and motels welcoming hunters to twenty-four-hour movies, toward the town of his wife's mother. Through sleet and wind-lashed rain and the sense that this travelling could be real as death. Towns buried or to be buried. Lakes whipped up in blackness inside a highway's elbow. Sharing coffee and an argument about how they always ended up in the same place, same dead end, familiar furnishings, edges of themselves blurring, afraid of losing themselves, night and journey already lost, radio a waterfall drowning a country song about something burning, lights wheeling across the windshield, phalanx of bubbles in foam flung south to north between and among and behind which dwelt a people deep in winter thought. Good summer. Best harvest in years. Lovely boy. Don't deserve it. Such luck. Going to be a long one and cold. You never can tell. Sweet child that was. Remember?

∞

Last night they were in the hottest pool. They were in the cave. They were in the hot pool again. A sweet voice keening a simple tune against the echo of more prosaic voices and the water's subterranean roar was joined by another in harmony. The owner of the first voice massaged the woman beside them as he was massaged by his wife who later would lie by his side untouched and confusing. Not as young as her voice indicated. The younger woman whose smooth shoulders received the massage then became masseur to her mother, if mother was correct, just as he became masseur to his wife, if wife was correct. Because that was the way of these things.

Pleasing symmetry, but false. Such debts ride in the belly a long time.

∞

Exhaustion overwhelmed them in Old Mother's living room on a thin mattress listening to comedy shows all night from the TV down the hall and the great thundering fridge cutting in and out. Here was a dream of watching TV girls on a tiny screen and coming a bit and coming gangbusters, waking to wet sheets in a hermetic room. A piss off. He was free to imagine anything at all and had to suffer these unprepossessing shrimps in girl uniform, dinky skirt and bra, chug chug chug, neck ache and aftermath of crashing semis, memory of blindness and fear.

Again, in an unfinished house, he gathered friends.

The stars still had no obligation.

His fear protected something so small.

His wife rose like a vampire, wrapped in something worse than solitude, veins flowing with new toxins. When would he wake up beside a corpse?

Slow creak of walker and footfalls down the hall, past the doorway, heavy body crossing, phone trilling, body eclipsed, breath moaning. Old Mother in nightdress laboured back and forth to answer phone, nature, door. Tiredness and pain tidal. In the kitchen the phone and pills. A long hall. At the opposite end bedroom and bathroom. Toilet seat a white plastic lifebuoy. Days ordered by the arrival of legbinders, bathers, cooks. Nights by pain, death fears, running dreams and gags.

He studied photographs and the help.

Young women most.

Studied his wife and her sisters as students and brides.

Sweet and cold.

Let's get these bandages on.

You know I heard sometimes animals are better than real mothers.

Laughtrack.

∞

They'd been driving through indigestible mountains. Saw a wolf quit its prey bloody by the road and step away, pausing often to look back. Bluebird nest boxes along the high highway. Ranch in the sagebrush. Dead houses. Ventures begun and abandoned. They argued. Arrived at the same place over and over, familiar set piece, barren little crossroads, she driving or he. This annual trip. He thinking everything all right; she thinking everything could be better. And now, unasleep in the hotsprings motel with the sense that everything is a line that no one will believe and every line is repeated and repeated, he can't put away the image of startled krill, the idea of a husband and wife working underwater. No one will believe the line he makes up but then why should it be believed since it's a line of defence, the shadow of a line. "I'm poisoning my wife, giving her small doses so no one will notice the slow deterioration." Or the metaphor's empty core. Been here before. Leaves in crisp piles stirring. Cool of October, clear rivers fogged by the smoking of mud in shallows instantly clear again, late afternoon decisions to make camp. Smell of cottonwoods, woodsmoulder, and a moment of whiskey silence at night before turning in. Awake at two, freezing, awake at dawn to strike the tent. Swelter and cool of car travel, imagejumbled, to this motel full of spooks, up astonished at two-thirty for this glass of water, dislocated, the page-turning impossibility of relaxation like a joke or does he mean possibility.

∞

They'd escaped briefly to take a drive through town.

I feel fuzzy, his wife said, shifting gear through a red light. Dreamed of taking an exam in an empty room. Didn't want to. Wanted sex. Wanted out.

He didn't interpret the dream though he could have, easily. Instead he listened and imagined he was a useful witness. To loss of skin tone, flexibility, memory.

What d'you think it means? he asked.

Not being here. Not being. Alone.

What?

I don't know what my mother wants.

Does she want anything?

She's got a funny way of wanting nothing.

She's refining her interests.

She's sad. She's completely vexing. You don't understand.

∞

And down again to Pompeii. He guilty, she dying.

Skeletons locked in mud and the archaeologist's reconstruction of event.

Once, in an unfinished house, he gathered friends.

Under heaven the stars had neither memory nor obligation.

His fear could have been diagnosed years ago.

Should he see a specialist?

The friends left without saying goodbye and he stepped through the framed wall beside the front door into the future. No conventional approaches for him, his passing stirred no one. Unfinished university degrees, sad terror of unemployment. He remembers his father on a ladder hanging Christmas lights while Mother looked on.

The floor is wet, she said. Over here the floor is wet.

Father fetched boards to place over the puddles. Cursing, he wrestled sheets of drywall from the top of a stack. Mother laughed nervously. Chunks of plaster crashed down.

The boy can't stop crying, she said. Poor child. He's shivering. Come and hold him. Come down and hold him.

☺

Old Mother and her daughter were crying. Seemed Old Mother's dearest friend, after a long struggle, had died of cancer. Recently they'd occupied different wings of the same hospital. They were born the same year in the same firehall and had lived and played together in the firemen's quarters above the horses.

That one who comes mornings she lives in that trailer park across from the cemetery, Old Mother said.

Does she, he said.

Got quiet neighbours.

I guess so.

Says she looks after this sixteen-year-old girl with cerebral palsy eleven till seven every day. Got to do everything. Girl can't talk or anything. Feeds her through a tube.

He couldn't tell if the noises she made were gasps or sighs or indicated pain or sadness. His wife sat on the floor, eyes shut. He screwed casters onto a coffee table and imagined twin deaths, him waking up in this packed house with no reason to stay.

What would you like for lunch? said his wife.

Got to make a lot of phone calls, said Old Mother. And she listed the names of the living who needed news of extinction.

Sandwich or soup? said his wife.

That would be nice, said Old Mother.

Which.

I don't mind. Anything would be nice. I'll have anything. You make what you like.

But what would you like?

I don't care, dear. Anything. Anything.

That afternoon he helped Old Mother arrange her week's supply of pills, stole a little blue pair of morphine, made a list of hardware stores from the yellow pages.

∞

Later, the masonry almost done and the house sealed, accidents still were possible, witness a visitor struck by a falling brick. Blood everywhere. He was sent next door for an ice pack to put on the broken head. Three big girls asked him for money. He supposed they were neighbours.

"I haven't got any."

They teased him about the way he walked. He emptied his pockets for them and the women gave him ice. A dog played in the yard. A baby. Played in dirt choked with thistles and tall weeds. A salesman arrived loudly and out there in the wild country made a deal with the oldest girl while the others all mocked him. At home ice melted and mixed with the victim's blood. Quite a sight.

∞

Sound of water from the bathroom nights it never got dark. Phone ringing. Sirens. Seemed they were evacuating everyone this side of the tracks on account of a derailment of tank cars carrying methane gas. Not to worry. Yellow sun came up clear anyway, casting long shadows down those wide streets, leaves like yellow chips whipped up in twisters, a metallic hurricane of shining ziplocs from the highschool, noise like a waterfall in the air overpowering traffic. Train on standby half a mile down the tracks, engineer chatting to a cop, TV crews hustling gear up the embankment. Smell of regular death gusting down from the feedlots north and east.

∞

He was in the neighbour's yard another time, sucking a long silver lollipop, when the girl came out with the salesman. They

43

picked their way over to a garden bench, mould-green wood, and she stepped one foot up and her skirt raised. She was laughing as the salesman talked and frowned, their eyes mysterious among the roses and lilies. Some deal, she said. She hauled red wax around her mouth. What can you expect? said the salesman. He slapped his thigh. The world ended.

∞

He dropped the morphine and strode out from Old Mother's house through town and along red paths atop coulee knuckles in October sunshine sweating like shrinkwrapped beef. A lookout bench above fort and river. Rail trestle stretched black a stagy horizon to the improvised battle raging below. He expected a female corpse on the bench. Expected red river trees instead of yellow. Dry mud to grab toes. Did not expect cactus discs in fizzing grass. Nor the morphine-blue sky. His fear drifted good and free just like the magpie floating down to the fort's garden patch to land on the pink-smocked flapping scarelady, a crucified corpse upended postplunge, while up here coyotes howled. Outside the bleached stockade a parking lot, tipi sticks, highway-crossed river, dunes of gumbo dried and runnelled by passing rain, and over all the blood of warriors. Good place for a fight, this. He imagined them, huge and feathered, bare-chested, fierce, unafraid, carrying mean-looking weapons. In the constant whish of traffic the rumble of a truck's shifting load was a comfort.

He walked by himself listening to himself curse the wind and wondered at the familiar strangeness of everything. Calm below the storm below the calm kind of thing. Entered hardware stores and drugstores and browsed aisles till town was an immense and brilliant display of artifacts he could only guess the use of.

∞

In the present he doesn't know. He thinks if memory's corruptible, maybe fear is mutable. He's impotent with shame and fear and envy. There's some light on the lake. He kneels on the floor, shivering. At dawn beside Pompeii he finds a selflit wristwatch with so many dials that he almost dies of excitement.

∞

Going down frequently to Old Mother's basement to clear space in the mouldy rumpus room, throw carpet over crumbling cement, fix least wobbly table, find chair with four legs, two awry, he'd established an office there among the junk. Set up a black-and-white TV, faint picture, no sound. A considered selection of old magazines from the stacks. Elbows on table, head in hands, he invented. He concocted. Memory and image. Mornings he compensated the weak daylight with a rickety floor lamp salvaged from the buckets and debris. The universe was younger than what was in it. There were sly wordless reaches he'd almost forgotten existed. In the basement, he shut his eyes. Winter was on its warpath, witness boiling leaves, wild prairie nightfall, hot lying colours. Canyon of no walls but starry darkness. Voices uttered sentences long and winding inside tight houses where weather was kept at bay and tracked by attractive women reading satellites in cities to the north. He felt himself becoming colourless and odourless. Woman and daughter poisoned by madman. Toward evening sun through high slit windows came on strong, then streamed.

There was a good moment one evening after playing cards (that firemen's convention deck all the gloss gone some girl stepping out of her grass skirt smiling forward tush reflected in a mirror behind), after Old Mother lost every hand but won the game and they were backing the wheelchair out of the dining room, a moment of complete remission. The chair got stuck. They were caught, the three of them. They'd sucked back such a lot of tea and pills.

Folks here have hard honest lives, Old Mother said.

Yes, he said.

They don't know anything but work, said his wife.

No one can find a job these days, said Old Mother.

45

No, he said.

I don't answer the door the way things are, she said. I keep my money at the bottom of the freezer. Under the oldest apples. I've made a list of valuables.

I have to pee, he said. Please let me out.

Here it is, she said. I keep it with me. Look at my handwriting. It makes me ashamed.

I really have to pee, he said, crossing his legs in front of Old Mother's bloated legs.

I have to pee too, she said. What are we going to do?

His wife collapsed against the wall laughing, and he couldn't help laughing, and Old Mother was laughing like a girl, wedged as she was in the threshold between them.

∞

Heading home by car, sipping coffee, still alive, leaving Old Mother to her slow and solo perambulations, they'd directed the same lives across the same borders, those same mountains, toward the coast, found themselves in the same places as before, steamy caves, elderberry groves, motels, in movie channel comedies also starring martial arts kids fighting video wars.

He feels himself trembling to escape the vortex engendered by his own fear, especially his fear of the fear of his wife of his own fear that closes him down. He's still gulping a glass of water in a motel room and it's still okay. Okay that he can't sleep. He's drinking water, turning away from the lake.

They've found in themselves and above dark matter. Nothing connecting but everything touching. No trespassing here except on business. Success no different than failure. Winners and losers gone shopping. Their day will come. He is this puzzle piece that engages with the puzzle of his wife and comes out clean. Gleaming flank of no one. Intricate, the way things meet. Where's the round thing with everything in it? No space left, the match perfect, suggestion of a whole wrong. Here are two entities. Dark. Light. Talk about how they work and get out of the basement. Tell a story about something else and a tunnel will appear, conduit from street to cellar, vent from foul to fresh air or fresh to foul. Another queasier joining.

Courtesy of?

Waiting for his wife to wake up, he has time to fill out a form regarding an ecological preserve and to read a Sam Beckett passage about a field, a great open space, slight downhill grade, distant horizon, blue sky and far-flung sun, grass uniformly green and every blade the same length. In the next room his wife has her eyes closed. He closes his and they both are coasting this long slope, an easy glide, breathing, not talking. At the pool they bend to drink, but the liquid's full of larvae which grow as they watch till bugs are crowding the milky water and beginning to leave in an ever-expanding glutinous exodus. They too are turning to jelly, starting to melt.

When his wife wakes up they discuss how they are always in the same place, all roads lead to Rome, here they are again, gridlock, etcetera. He tells her how terrific she looks and she tells him not to sound so surprised.

He supposes silence might be construed as a statement of love, suggests it to his wife.

Do you love me? she says.

You're fishing again.

What else can I do? You never say a plain word.

I don't know.

Do you even like me?

Saddened and downcast they get dressed and try to make peace and are barely on the road again before they reach home.

꩜

Dark. Quiet. Raining.

She unpacks their belongings and makes the bed while he contemplates the familiar set of lights across the deep black valley. Gillhung fish dead in a still net. Scales of a carp sleeping in shadows. Over the stainless sink he cleans the label off a can of beans, feeling as calm as sodden leaves yet with fury flames licking his skin as if all the running built up in his body these recent times of travelling fast, somewhere to go, counting miles between points, hoarding up the anger of speed, have got hold of every nerve. Doesn't want to talk or be looked at. He works the sharp lid back and forth till it clicks loose from the can and watches lovemakers through invisible branches of winter trees in duet and alone commit themselves to a strange state. Comatose, preoccupied, untethered. Especially the soloists, vapid-visaged, half-asleep, the inner eye controlling the inner life. Almost meets himself there. Then the mopping up of fluids, shot muscles, sleep. They are terrified, not merely frightened. Mirrorlike these intermissions. The skin of his hand turns cool in an aching wave, a sudden spill. Looks down. The sharp lid has made a circle of surging blood. Surprising strength of this grasp, the jagged pain of unclenching, scalloped edges coming out of flesh, unsticking. Dull red heart beating under the cold tap. Water heating for tea, one cup, two cups. Nothing realer than this, not wanting to be seen to say a word, no word to say, but looking at her small hands and thinking all's not well.

# Salvage

## 1. THE VILLAGE

Glynis Tilley rises before daylight. It's her birthday. She picks dripping berries beside the highway. All spring she's watched crows take the long strands of hair she saved from her brush and each morning secured under the window along the sill outside her bedroom. Now she sleeps away the morning on the sundeck and dreams about a perfect underwater community, in a cool shallow blue coral lagoon; she'll wake burning, feverish, thinking, This is the hour of my birth seventeen years ago.

Patrick drives in from the north, Clarence from the south. To be accurate, only Patrick is driving; Clarence's wife chauffeurs her husband. She's promised to help Mrs Travis with the preparations. Patrick has the windows up and the air conditioner on; the Mahler symphony he's listening to makes him think of demerara sugar. He's wearing knee-length shorts, a clean white shirt, and black plastic cat's-eye sunglasses. He's exultant. He has butterflies.

Clarence's wife steers with her right hand, cups her left into the wind to dry her armpit and says she's not looking forward to this.

Clarence has butterflies. He feels guilty. He's wearing an old green paint-spattered track suit. "Jogging suit," he murmurs.

"Why is it you always mumble when I'm driving? You speak clearly when you're driving, you're much better company, much more alert. You said you didn't want to drive. I asked you twice."

"What are you not looking forward to, Sandra?" Clarence stares at his wife's profile. He thinks: I must try to think.

"To this Travis thing. I hate these pleasant social rituals. They're so *nice*."

"If I remember correctly, you volunteered." Quite simple: will we make love? This morning? How and where? Will I tell?

"Last year when it was over I was so relieved—I loved everybody out of relief. That's when Mrs Travis signed me up. Are you aware it's twelve kilometers from town to our place? You're out of shape, you'll die in this heat."

"Closer as the man jogs."

"What?"

"As the man jogs, I said. As the crow flies . . . closer."

"You really wanted to drive, didn't you? Christ, why didn't you at least wear shorts?"

"Too vulnerable." Clarence gazes out at the summer sky, high streaky clouds. He supposes he will have to run home, at least part way. He'll think more clearly then; *afterward, alone,* he can decide what to do. Keep lying. He'll get Pat to drop him off at the farmer's cut. Sandra deserves some consideration. Suddenly he hears the tires on the sticky road, the engine roaring—wake up! —sees from the corner of his eye his wife easing the gas; his heart pounds; the car by degrees is entering a strange seamless landscape; clouds leave the brown farmland for sun to etch fences into; he's acutely conscious of his fingers rolling a ball of fuzz he's absently picked from the track suit.

Sandra's thinking how indolent the countryside seems on weekends, how she usually likes going to the village, but this morning hates the idea.

On Saturdays and Sundays town is a completely different place than on week days. Traffic licks along steel roads instead of rumbling over rough tarmac, and men walk slowly down side streets letting their cars dry in the sun. Cotoneasters buzz more lazily. Air enough for everyone under the leaf-spinning oaks, and today it's dustfree. Teens jump skateboards on and off curbs. Crows scream all morning as the Mrs Banks Ramsey Mays Skrivanos Potts Sinclair fix bowls of salad or roll hamburgers in their kitchens, all doors and windows open, radios playing. This afternoon the Travises are having their annual potluck. Blankets on the front lawn for the kids, deckchairs front and back. The shady back reserved for those who want a quieter meal, the baby boomers who will leave their children to the care of grandparents at the front. Mr Travis built a new fence this spring and youngsters clutching hot dogs will climb from it into the plum trees. Mrs Travis as usual will worry for her annuals, her roses. Her husband will hide the broken buds, the snapped and fallen plum branches. She will discover the wilting pile behind the gazebo on Monday morning.

It rained in the night and the graffiti on the bridge's stone buttresses have washed off—all the swastikas, rock groups, sex parts have been erased, even from the underbelly of the bridge. Mr Travis at breakfast speaks excitedly about the discovery of the sunk Titanic. The sun pushes up, pushes up, steam rising everywhere, such a smell of green, pavements drying; later it will press down, horizon fading, town flattened. The Travis yard populated with voices. "Imagine coming across it! Seeing it in front of you, still upright, as if sailing still, like the iceberg was a bad dream!"

The whole town woke at dawn, a single male house finch singing loud about the last rain last eastbound clouds; nestling crows learning deserted parking lots, unlidded trash bins. Sun pushing. Glynnis Tilley picking berries.

Patrick finishes Mahler in the McDonald's parking lot while watching the road along which Clarence will soon appear. He pretends to stumble for the first time on the thought that

Clarence probably believes this meeting an assignation. He smiles and lightly slaps the dash. He's twenty-seven and blowing law school—he must be because he's not worried, not living on nerves; he sleeps well, bounces out of bed mornings. He will expose Clarence. Delicious. Only the most depressed, round-shouldered, weary students do excellently. He's having too good a time. He enjoys school, likes his professors. He's been flirting with Clarence since term began. At first a kind of knee-jerk reaction to the older man's attention, but now he turns charm on and off, playing the hunter. He tracks with a finger a fly crawling outside the windshield. Purses his lips. The world is deeply sick, according to what he has witnessed Clarence doing. St Vitus Dance at Swan Lake. He's lived with it for months—it's the fly in the ointment, interfering with his happiness, the fly in the movie, the fly in the web, half-human, half-beast, Help me, help me! He's always known he'd have to do something. He'd like to heal things up, but finds himself rehearsing blackmail. Sombre and malignant, that image, the figure of a man with a mannequin. Think mannequin for corpse. Prettify the scene: branch tips ripple the water: a brooding dark sort of beauty where pity is all for the beast, not for the idiot human.

"Hello, Mrs Travis."

"Hi, Sandra. Going to be a fine day. Oh good, you brought your famous garden bowl. I'm so mad. Mr Travis promised he'd bring out the chairs. Now he's stuck in the garage with his damn train set. Would you be a dear? He'll pay attention to you."

"Where are the others?"

"Oh, along shortly, I dare say."

Sandra walks under trees like deep drapery across the back lawn to the garage. Through the dusty window she sees Mr Travis astraddle a cluster of houses in a valley, one leg on a bridge, the other on a granite mountain. He looks up as she enters. Together they manoeuvre the stepladder to a bare patch of floor at the centre of the rail system. Sandra climbs up, yanks the deckchairs from the rafters and passes them to Mr Travis.

She thinks he's looking at her midriff when her tank top lifts. In fact he's delighted at the tiny perfect windows, one each eye in the grey beside the pupil, as she bends toward him with the chairs. Dust gets in her nose and she sneezes. He tells her to hold tight. Quickly, she reviews her life.

She was born on the outskirts of Toronto thirty-five years ago, had five lovers before meeting Clarence when she was twenty-six. She was reluctant to move out west, to this part of the country, where Clarence was born. She had three miscarriages. Clarence is forty-seven. Her nose is dripping. She wipes her fingers on her shorts and leaves grey smudges on the carefully pressed cotton. They've been here eight years. She's always prided herself on being organized, on allowing for the unexpected, on reserving time for the making of lists, on keeping as much as possible to the deadlines she sets herself. Clarence has admired these qualities in her.

Mr Travis takes her arm as she descends. He's trying to find the right words to ask her how it felt up there: did she feel like a god, did she think how her sneeze would be thunder to the little people below? But she's out of the garage before he can say a thing. He turns off the little engine that's been bravely circling all the time they were on the ladder.

"It's about time!"

"Morning, Patty. Sandra drove me. Let's sit in the car a minute. I need to catch my breath. I've run two blocks. I'm supposed to be jogging home. Lord knows."

"You look cute. Like a little furry blue bear. Poor old Clarence. Let's go in. I'm starved."

"Not yet. Please. Put some music on if you like. I just need a moment to sit and think."

Mr Travis secretly wants to be a salvage diver, wants to fly with the tide over that great wreck. On his way from the garage to the house, he stops to pull some weeds. Ethiopia, says the radio voice from the next yard, then in a jocular tone of voice begins the weather. Mr Travis has a newscast in his head; he's down at that great ship lost for so long between the old and new world, and he finds a country of starving children in the hold. He lets the current carry him, lower him into the richly appointed cabins full of princess dolls. His fingers riffle the unspoiled pink limbs to reveal smooth flax-studded loaves of bread; the blue doll eyes study him with mild curiosity as he empties his lungs to descend further.

Clarence and Patrick sit at a bench in McDonald's and talk about *Carmina Burana*. Patrick, who's involved, says the current production still has openings in the chorus. And Clarence, plastic knife tearing through scrambled eggs into a styrofoam plate, his teeth on edge, thinks this a devious and somehow appropriately immoral way of getting out of the house regularly, at least for a few months. As a younger man, he sang with a choir whose principals were graduate students in performance at the university where he was studying law. Rehearsals took place biweekly in the auditorium. He imagines the performance nights as ironically sad affairs, by which time certainly this relationship will have run its course. Bitter suite.

"What are you grinning at?"

"The course of our lives set to *Carmina Burana*."

"Want to hear a funny story?" Patrick asks.

December that year Clarence and Patrick and Sandra are living thousands of miles apart.

Patrick lies on the floor of his uncle's study. He's looking after the house in Sevenoaks, a short ride from London into the Kent countryside, while his uncle is in Italy concluding a lawsuit involving a prominent banker. Patrick's family has decided Patrick has suffered a nervous breakdown—why else would he quit school, in midstride, so to speak? Patrick takes the train into London every dreary morning. He's been to the Tower, Charles Dickens's house, Westminster Abbey, the London Museum, the National Gallery. Each afternoon he reads the American and Canadian papers. The damp air smells of mould; the sun hasn't shone properly since he arrived. He's looking for news of Clarence, which when he finds it will enable him to return to Canada and his studies; he'll have money to spend; he'll be able to breathe more easily. He and London wait, as if at the bottom of the ocean. Across Regents Park or along the Embankment he believes men are following him. At night his dreams are homosexual and violent; often he is mutilated. He's in love with nobody, though wouldn't mind being in love if the right person came along, the one of his dreams. He rolls on his back. The ceiling of his uncle's study is blue and ornate, with a raised design in gold that resembles lattice work. It's like being in a gold cage. Exactly like being in a gold cage.

Clarence is living under an assumed name in a highway motel in Virginia; even now, as he's about to pack his bags one more time before meeting his Miami contact, the police are closing in. He is drinking Old Crow, chainsmoking Camels. When he was fifteen he fell in love for the first time, with Alf the cigarette salesman. But Alf loved a local girl, one of two orphaned sisters. Outside Clarence's motel room the farmland looks white and squashed, as though some exhausted leviathan had rested there a second. It has started to snow. Just before moving with his family to Toronto, just before his sixteenth birthday, he stood on the shore of the lake and watched Alf watching a police diver bring a body to the surface. Alf stood apart from the main group of onlookers. Clarence couldn't think of a thing to say. He'd never spoken to the man, knew this would be the last opportunity for them to meet. He knew that. Alf could have been playing harmonica, something bluesy. Alf could have stood there crying. Alf could have taken off his clothes and waded out. Alf could have told his story. Clarence had come to recognize the drawl in the corner store when Alf talked cigarettes to the storekeeper, longed to hear it now. Out on the lake they were slipping on the body bag. The body used to belong to the girl Alf loved. Clarence believes he's as downcast down on his knees, broken as Alf was then. And like Alf he too, alone in his motel room, is upright, quiet and dry-eyed. Out on the highway ghostcars are assembling.

"That's not very funny."

"I saw you dump the body."

"And what about Sandra? What do you have in mind for Sandra?"

"December, Sandra will be pregnant, so not completely unhappy."

Glynis Tilley has a sunburnt face. She looks at her parents and imagines them nervous and young. They were twenty-two and twenty-three when she was born—her mother only five years older than Glynis is today! Dad is mowing the lawn, running the machine back and forth in parallel lines, fence to house, his face serious, worry lines in his forehead. Mom's in the kitchen baking pastry for pies for the Travis affair. Glynis leans on the sundeck railing and watches her father down in the yard. The deck is off the master bedroom—*their* room. Glynis steps barefoot into the house, onto the soft rug by her parents' bed, passes through the room and down the hall. Her body still carries the sensation of gliding underwater, a slow walk across the sandy floor of a lagoon; her mouth still remembers the early morning berries, sweet and cool and wet with rain. She feels the house round her like the whole world, wants to tell someone, wants to say something so vital it would be like a good disaster, earth-shaking. She paces room to room, looking out each window, touching each sill. She's sailing through time, to be in love, to love someone, to pitch her life against another life, other lives, to love friends. The trees change in front of her; the streets wrap boulevards and squeeze grass toward the light; and light presses down, covers the front of her body. "What are you doing?" asks her mother. "Nothing." She's framed in the window, silhouette from inside, all detail from the street. Her father waves, but she just stands there. A rocket, trembling, soon she'll take off. He mows the lawn, back and forth, back and forth, facing her, then away. She tries another window. The back yard looks dark and cool; a cat crosses; she counts four butterflies. Another window. Back and forth, shirtless. Another. Fingertips on sill, mind humming, she's in a trance. Another. Another.

Maybe Patrick saw the body, saw Clarence put the body into the lake, maybe. But one thing's sure, Patrick didn't see Nadine, didn't see the girl. No one saw Clarence pick up the girl—he made sure of that, waiting till long after the bar rush, till streets were nearly empty, till no cars were in sight and she stood alone on the corner, till she wandered down from the corner, stamping her little boots because it was cold. Till he felt calm and fatal. Till that moment when night seems to stop. Till doing one thing is as easy as doing another, and doing something is essential. The act of shifting from park to drive, touching the gas, feeling nervous as the filament in a shattered light bulb. Memory disconnects. He can't see anything but the girl, feel only his wallet, hear her voice certain and practiced, the transaction. Chunks of time, gasoline circles. Pulling her long hair. Examining her place. Pushing her into the rainbow. She laughing like a harmonica, he mustn't show emotion. Pulling up beside her rolling down the window looking at her face wiping off her makeup making love to circles. Fingers slick with gasoline from the surface. Till now.

"Is everything ready, Sandra? They'll be here soon. Everybody's coming. And it's turned out such a glorious day. The chairs. The blankets. The barbecues. Tables and tablecloths. Napkins. Cutlery. Glasses. Paper plates. My trifles, your garden bowl. Marshmallows. The fireworks the Christmas lights (if they stay past dark). Oh the fruit punch! Mr Travis? The bread the cake the party hats the games—front and back—the driveway clear the street clear invitations all sent. Signs on the flower beds, garage locked. First aid kit. Bathroom cleaned, map on the back door. Garden tools and poisons locked away. All doors except the back door, and all windows, locked. Supervisors appointed, entertainment arranged, and I think we've done it! Are you ready, Sandra?"

"Mrs Travis, I'm ready to drop. I don't know where you find the energy."

"You'll see. When everyone's here you'll get your second wind."

"So you saw me. What did you see, Patrick? What is it you want?"

"It's rather cliché, Clarence. Guess."

"You're kidding. Money?"

"It's been almost six months. I'd say that given my silence you were safe. I've felt my stock go up every week."

"How much."

"Quarter mill."

"When."

"Four weeks."

"If I don't pay?"

"Four weeks from today, my lawyer has instructions to open an envelope in a safety deposit box. Needless to say, in the event of anything happening to me—disappearance, death, etcetera—the box will be opened immediately."

"If I do pay on time?"

"You get the document, my promise of silence, and I'll leave the country."

"Wouldn't I follow you and kill you to guarantee that silence?"

"A clause in my will will give the number of another box. If I die naturally the envelope inside will be destroyed."

"A natural death could be arranged."

"Well, that's where risk comes in."

"I'd have to trust you to call it a day after the two-fifty? Trust you not to go to the police anyway?"

"You have no choice."

"My dear Patrick, I didn't do it. If pushed I will admit I knew the girl. *Sandra* knew the girl. It would be embarrassing, but that's all."

"If the police started dragging—"

"They'd find nothing."

"I'm sure the station wagon—"

"Gone to the wreckers to become a run of shiny new toaster ovens."

"Are you certain?"

"You're bluffing."

"You left your mark on the scene, Clarence. It's still there to be pointed out."

"Nonsense. Erle Stanley Gardner."

"Test me."

"Listen, Patrick. *You* want to hear a funny story?"

December of that year nothing has changed, except *Carmina Burana* has been performed in front of appreciative if small audiences. And Sandra feels smug and happy. She is indeed pregnant. The Nadine episode was the last of its kind. She sits in the hall at the final concert and looks at Clarence, her new slim husband, and for now is not troubled that they seldom make love. She thinks of Nadine only fleetingly: Nadine was necessary for Clarence and her because they couldn't do anything by themselves and she would not tolerate another man. That Nadine actually died the last night they saw her was mere coincidence, had nothing to do with Sandra or Clarence; it did not touch Sandra at all, though Clarence later spoke to her of a sign, of a feeling of guilt. The suspected relationship between Patrick the young law student tenor and her husband has either naturally ended or was all along a product of her imagination. They sing side by side in suits. If not for the music they would be absurd. The lights are low, and they are all in the tavern, having passed through springtime on the meadow; soon will come the court of love.

Clarence gazes out from McDonald's at the summer sky, high streaky clouds. He will run part way home, has to think more clearly, must decide what to do. Keep lying. Pat is saying he'll drop him at the farmer's cut. Perhaps the rain washed the graffiti from the stone bridge. Imagine jogging under, seeing the bridge overhead in the dark rain of a night run, curved and ancient as if sailing above you; you're on a treadle at the bottom of an ocean, and the belly of the bridge is bleached like an iceberg in a dream!

The Travis yard throngs, populated with voices. The inhabited trees change; the streets wrap boulevards and squeeze grass toward the light, and light presses down, pushes down, covers the front yard. "What are you doing?" "Want to hear a funny story?"

Mr Travis stops the party. Crows cease grumbling to look down at the stunned guests. They have all misunderstood.

Silence. A slow turning of heads. A distant sprinkler goes sht-sht-sht-sht . . . What Travis really said, so excitedly, was nothing much. He was just so pleased at having something to say at all that it exploded from him with an epiglottal clap. "Twenty percent of the world's population consume eighty percent of the world's resources." The guests think he is announcing war and cannibalism. Some understand that eighty women have been raped by twenty men. That twenty missionaries have eaten eighty natives. That eighty Third-World countries have declared war on twenty industrial nations. That twenty bull terriers are afraid of eighty chihuahuas. That eighty whites can contract tuberculosis from twenty blacks. That of a hundred people eighty are wrong, and none of the twenty right have the resources to make any difference. That some miracle food costs eighty dollars and twenty cents an ounce, but an ounce could feed two thousand and eighty of the world's starving for the rest of their lives.

This is the whole family on pause, in the Travis yard, eighty in the hot front, twenty in the cool rear. *O Fortuna!* Like children in church, they make faces. The motionless kids and grandads itch and sweat, yearn to scratch. The old ladies are as loose as they'll ever be. Everyone longs to get naked. Parents anxious in the long shocked lull roll their eyes. All is horrible and wonderful for that moment, till Mrs Travis clears her throat for her husband, folds her arms, opens her mouth. And relief falls like a shroud, life resumes with a shout, when Mrs Travis makes things clear.


2. MISS ARMSTRONG AND NADINE

I drowned in the lake.

The lake got me, too.
I paddled out on my back on a brilliant day in May.

The man dumped me from his station wagon in January, and it sure wasn't hot, wasn't cool, wasn't bright.

Thirty years ago.

This year. Like I said, January.

I was thinking of the sky as a belly, me floating inside, my own belly afloat, a buoy, me fastened to it, wanting loose.

Nobody thought about me, no one, water made my skin real white, my throat swelled up and mud got between my legs.

I suddenly felt calm, not crazy, fingers moving ripples against my thighs, sunset, beating, can a horizon be upside down?

Why? Who cares? It's just nerves, only the suck of the mud, some stupid arm lifting by itself to these blind eyes, to shield them. I figured it was always night in the world, so in the lake, what else?

Imagine us meeting this way.

Imagine us meeting at all.

Nadine, this is Judy, my daughter.

Hi, Judy Armstrong.

Judy won't speak, Nadine. She can't. She's my angel. I was in love with her father, you understand, he left, you've heard the story. Look at the pike nosing through the reeds. I considered the bone-handled bread knife before I decided on the lake, but to spill my blood would have been to spill hers. Look, he's a dark torpedo in deep shadows. His tail flickers. I am the school of fingerlings lazy as a cloud above. It's in me to be afraid, but to do nothing. All my life, nothing. My sister's name is Bea and she lives at the lake edge still. The day Judy and I finally swam we changed the lake into a hive, so she cannot leave, Aunt Bea, worker bee, she's not left in thirty years. Miss Armstrong, Miss Armstrong. The two Miss Armstrongs are receiving. Who is the letter for, who the phone call? She walks round the lake at least once a week, knows the kingfisher, the woodpecker, the swallows. At this season the swallows in their hundreds dance for insects a world beyond our silver one, and the mortal Miss Armstrong, blinded by sun, loses count; she tries to hold the sky's reflection. A murder-suicide? she considers, suicide-murder? but is still not sure. Accidental death by drowning. But wilful in any case; she will never forgive the lake, her sister, the year. Even while the memory fades—and each spring it has faded, five, ten, fifteen, twenty, twenty-five— she continues to blame me who being immortal can absorb or give back nothing but bubbles of air. Miss Armstrong in your walking shoes, in your rubbers in winter, Miss plain Armstrong, Miss dull Armstrong, brittle as your stick as you circle the lake, do you know I will soon be too big to hold?

The lake bottom is like streets at night, the night streets of all the cities I've walked, different from day streets. Black absorbs light, they taught that in school. The lake bottom is like broken sponge. I tried to bake my own birthday cake when I was ten. Eggs and butter and sugar, a pound cake in a Bundt pan. I didn't figure to grease the pan and the cake came out broken. The smell of a birthday is cake burning. Traffic headlights sink into a dark that smells of Chanel, cigarettes, and sex. If I want to start laughing, I pull my hair hard as I can. This splits me from other people, they think I'm crazy. I will never be twenty, Miss Armstrong. I came to this drowned place the same way I used to step from the sidewalk, the same way you put yourself on the lake surface thirty years ago, in a dream, knowing but not thinking about sacrifice, about futility. But I'm not like you, I kicked and scratched to stay alive; you fought to drown. When he pulled my hair, I laughed and he damn near stopped. Nadine, Nadine, he shouted over and over (I always used my own name, not like other girls). He wanted me to quit laughing so he could keep hurting. He called me back, each time from some small room farther and farther away. Laughs came out like chunks of buttery black cake, not the shining bubble laughs I laughed in daylight but absorbent ones, soaking up the light in his eyes.

Nadine, I'll never be twenty either. Words come easy here because they are all we have. You get used to not breathing. We've all the time we need for happiness, to just enjoy each other, to be patient and thoughtful. You say something, I say something, you say something. You can touch a finger to your lips and sit under a plane tree at the most dappled table on the sunniest boulevard in Paris. Let out a story when the right words are waiting.

Sorry, Miss Armstrong, I don't get it.

We're dead. Your fingers don't push, do they, child? Feet don't kick, teeth won't chew? Any migraine, any worry?

I can't touch my lips because I don't know where they are, my fingers won't stay still, won't stay together.

It's like that at first. Imagine a single bloom in a cluster of honeysuckle. Imagine a rosebud beginning to relax. Imagine a breeze swings the reaching honeysuckle toward the rose.

I'd rather be back drinking coffee on the corner in the middle of winter trying to look sexy in a parka and legwarmers with my knees knocking together and goosebumps zipping up and down my spine.

Hard edges, dear. Let go of fences and phone lines and sewers and roads and rails and flight routes. Here everything is muted, you can go anywhere. A late afternoon in August. White-clothed tables laid out across a big field by the sea. Ladies and gentlemen gliding between. The brine-bitten coast of a seventeenth-century Italian estate. Waiters dressed in brocade, men with fine legs in cream stockings, we ladies wearing long gowns of cunningly damasked cotton trimmed with Nottingham lace over pongée silk undergarments. The whole party anticipates news of the war. An officer, slightly drunk, is about to reveal to an acquaintance some intrigue with a certain lady of our group.

I left a whole fridge full of food. I was living with a chick I really dug. I quit coke. I just bought a new TV. I was saving for a car. I had a regular who wanted to take me to Hawaii.

Bea liked television but I thought it pathetic, a hoax, a poor substitute.

So, you been to those places, then, Miss Armstrong? To Italy and Paris?

Given a stronger current, we could be under the Seine with casks of napoleons and the skeletons of royalty.

Look at Judy floating near the surface, it's bright there, I guess she's watching the moon. She's cute. She keeps sticking her nose into the air, making ripple shadows. You haven't really been anywhere, have you?

She likes the shallows, especially when there's boats, likes them to churn through her. She shatters, then comes together again. She had a wonderful time when they were dragging the lake for you.

I guess. I don't like this, feeling totally spaced out.

Isn't she beautiful in this light? She shimmers. Judy's never lived in the world. She's always been drifting. Like frog spawn, like weed. I've lived in the world, you've lived in the world, that's where we've lived. Now we're dead in the lake. Dead in the water. I've longed for someone to talk to, someone to see my daughter. I hoped another person would drown.

I didn't drown, I was already dead.

Well, you're here, and I'm glad, that's all that counts. We can't be the same just because we're both dead. I'm glad you're here. Shall we take the grand tour?

Strut our stuff, Miss Armstrong? Hey, I don't even know where my stuff all is.

Take my arm, Nadine. You know that all the waters on earth are connected, that except for small mineral differences, all water is the same. Everything alive is made of water, even the driest rock contains a little water. When winter comes the snow hisses on the lake. If you put your ear to the surface you can hear it hissing. Hail rings like church bells, and rain and sleet tick like a clock.

You mean there are tunnels for the water to come in and go out?

Everything is connected, joined.

So you mean we can go other places? We don't have to stay in this lake? We can swim away, go on trips, visit rivers, cross the ocean and be with whoever we want?

As if that. Though I admit I've been afraid that Judy so close to the surface might evaporate.

Can we be ice and steam? Can we be clouds? Can we rain? Can we be lapped by animals, turned into milk, into strawberries, watermelon, corn? Can we bake? Can we be stale cake? Can we be strawberry shortcake? Strawberries and cream? Can we sit in someone's basement and turn into beer? Can we get a guy drunk, a living man in a bar in some city, a depressed and frustrated guy about to commit murder, can we get a guy like this too drunk to move? Can we climb through roots into enormous trees? Can we turn green?

Nadine, you are charming, utterly charming. Wait. This is a fine café. Let's rest under the awning and order some petit fours. I think we may even indulge in a small cognac. It's been a full afternoon; you look a little pale. We shall quietly sit and watch. That faint rumbling is highway traffic on the bridge. Take no notice. I pretend it's Mount Fuji snoring.

∽

I'm thinking about sex. It's funny I don't know why but I can't stop going over and over it. Bodies together. Parts of bodies covering, going into other parts of bodies. Eggs growing inside female bodies. Bits of fishy sperm growing inside male bodies. New bodies sometimes growing inside female bodies. And it's like a movie, little flashes of light going off all over. It kind of tickles, makes me want to sneeze, you know what I mean? But I can't sneeze, I'm beginning to feel kind of fabulous, we're free, aren't we? No more bodies, no more rooms, no more windows. Do you feel like this? Miss Armstrong?

Sorry, sugar. I wasn't listening. You were saying?

I was just thinking, Miss Armstrong, it's great about no more sex, isn't it? That it's over?

Oh yes. That gentleman to whom I was referring—the intrigue with a certain lady?—well, listen. The business suit, the sun hat. Singapore. European jewel trader, 1916. He looks rather bemused. He's obviously fleeing unpleasant memories—let's see. It's his father's mistress in Holland he's in love with. You can well believe he'll have problems to face when he goes home. What with the twins and one albino and the mistress's confession of the secret wedding to the father, the father's vengeful undermining of the son's business ventures in England.

Doesn't he seem forlorn, the poor man. Smitten by the intolerable heat, exhausted from a recent bout of malaria. He's also currently in love—as in love as a white can be with a native—with his favourite servant, a sixteen-year-old Malay boy. And as you observe, they are obviously intimately involved. Such a sad smile as he takes the hand of the certain lady's husband; everybody in the company is convinced that he's her lover, by inclination if not in fact. The husband looks daggers, apoplectic purple; our hero smiles through, oblivious. He's thinking of the Malay. He's thinking once again how amazingly like his new Dutch wife is the wife of this husband. How gentle and laughing and fey she is. Du Pré, jolly good to see you, we must take the shade, he says. Du Pré splutters and strides away. Strange fellow, why did he do that? All the company stares. Alas, there is nothing we can do but show sympathy by lowering our eyes.

Salut, Miss Armstrong, cheers. You're nuts, but I like you.

Memories are our only walls, Nadine. My own man was a cowboy, rode rodeo, cigarette salesman for the district. We met once a week for more than a year through 1956, 1957. His name was Alf James. I swam out on his twenty-ninth birthday, May 29, 1958. I swam twenty-nine strokes, twenty-nine and twenty-nine and twenty-nine. I cried that man a river, made the river a lake, made the lake a screen. He was James Dean in *Rebel Without a Cause*, I was Natalie Wood. I could have sent that man a rose, I would have borne that man a child.

Well, I've been on the pill long as I can remember. I never met anyone I wanted to get pregnant by. Mother was very particular, always said soon as I started to bleed, she'd put me on the wheel. First I liked sex. In the beginning it was money and favours and rock and roll and power and glory, amen. It was something else. But that got boring, it got so I couldn't care less one way or the other. I mean with nice guys it was nice and all, but nothing lasted, I mean then it was easy to take, folk music, nice melody, no guts.

You're finding your depth, I can tell.

When I was a kid we lived next to a gentle sad couple who never ever left their broken-down house and had no children of their own. I spent hours looking into their yard. They had all kinds of flowers and they sat there in the flowers in wooden chairs, always smiling. Ate breakfast lunch and supper outside with chopsticks. They were together most of the time, but real quiet, they only talked in whispers. They looked happy. I wanted to be their kid, I wanted to be with them. Then the guy built a fence and they and their house disappeared, I don't remember anything about them for years after that, till I got tall enough to see over the fence. Everything was different. The place had gotten full of weeds, and though they were still together I could hear what they said, and what they were saying to each other was weather and bitching and sarcastic, and they seemed old and sick and worn out.

Very good.

I want to move, do something. I feel kind of nervous, punchy. How come you're not nervous? You know how water stays fresh? There's a flow. This lake must have a source.

It comes from a little stream in the marshy place where skunk cabbage grows. I'll show you.

I know you say there's no borders here, but I feel like I felt when the fence went up. Or worse: like I would have felt if I'd known I'd soon lose the couple so happy in their yard for good. Maybe what I used to know and feel hasn't gone, maybe I just keep forgetting it—but that's really bad because remembering hurts, you've got to lose everything all over again.

Here's the marsh. Reach out and put your hand in a cabbage flower. Feels yellow, huh? Cold and yellow. The underground stream is full this time of year. Women are happy, Nadine, generally we are pretty happy. We have a knack for happiness that most guys don't have.

Oh sure. We got bounce, we are big-hearted, humming a song or tapping a foot most of the time, we got natural good spirits. Nothing we can't nail down, step back from and laugh at. Nothing depresses us for long. We swerve at sadness, refuse to despair. We don't let our fingers do the walking. When our heart breaks, when our sweety's ill, our kid lost, grampa confused, we don't call a tow truck, we don't call the cops or an ambulance. While our hands are busy, we keep shining like a lighthouse on whoever wants to sail on home, sometimes we get weak from giving strength where we can, sometimes we pass out we're so filled with happiness, we can't touch, can't even look without bawling our eyes out, without falling in love. We fall in love over and over, every day with a different person. We hurt, we are too gentle and soft, our happiness is a soft gentle light, it will stab the hell round us.

And if some cowboy tries to make sense of us we are anyway still safe, Nadine, ahead of the game, we can twist the poor soul round our finger. If some cigarette salesman thinks he can use our words himself, he's wrong, he can't. He can only sell what he's got in his little case, because he knows selling. He can't see what we've done, what we're capable of, no salesman can see beyond what he's selling, what his daddy back in Virginia sold.

And us, we're filled with happiness. You're out of this world, lady. After sex most salesmen just play guitar or show pictures of their families.

Babies.

Right. Sometimes babies.

You and I, Nadine, we are swimming ghosts, a kind of aspic for his children.

I don't know. Let's go upstream as far as we can.

We can't. Something terrible will happen. I don't want to. Don't be bitter, Nadine. Something horrible will happen. We'll stay here, we won't move. It's all in not wanting to hurt anyone. We'll stay looking at the surface. Silver silver silver silver...

Look, Judy's playing in the reeds by the opening. Coming, Judy? Be cool, Miss Armstrong. We'll swim through together.

Silver silver...

Miss Armstrong, it'll be great.

Too dangerous. There's a man in Nairobi Kenya in love with a South African woman, a woman escaped from the townsites of Joberg, a woman once loved by the son of a white South African from Pretoria, a university boy who helped her to escape to have his baby far away. In a village in Korea a man is going to leave everything, his cattle his inheritance his family his future. He will take only the love that he's fallen into. In a desert of jagged rocks two monkeys are licking each other, travelling, fighting each other, moving on, sleeping together. They make a nest of warm stones to curl into at night. The desert is filled with rock patterns in their shape. She dies and he travels round and round breaking the moulds to forget. One day a Spaniard sees a fire burning in the distance. Everyone killed in the war leaves behind an outline needing to be smudged. Everywhere something terrifying is about to happen. Men in airplanes shoot people on the ground. Back home they are gentle gentle gentle with their wives. In France a monk. Bamboo fingernails. Trade spiral. Counter revolution. A tall woman wearing scarlet feathers in her headdress drives an ox. A man is driven, the people are driven. Call this time the middle, early middle, late middle, new middle. Stay here. Stay and listen. Going goes nowhere except going. Call this the lake, call this the dead man's float, call this treading water.

Miss Armstrong, I want to be with people, close as I can get. There's something someplace I can do, a tiny push that probably won't make any difference to anything, but it's physical, nothing like memory or imagining. I'm not like you, I can't stay here and float.

You can't get close. You can't even get close.

Maybe I can. If I want.

Blood means water, Nadine. That's the secret of death. Listen. We have all the blood we need here. We flow through it, not it through us.

You said you wanted someone to talk to. You were glad I came. Maybe there'll be others, shouldn't we try to find others? I want to be around people. Dead or alive doesn't matter.

Others. No. There are no others.

Miss Armstrong.

I'm weary. I don't feel quite myself.

We gotta do something, Miss Armstrong.

Lukewarm. Stuck. Tepid. Stuck.

Miss Armstrong, it's because you make things up. We can swim right out of here. It won't be hard.

Stuck.

It's easy, come on, think of freezing, think of boiling, that's all you need do. I'm going.

Another way of saying there's an American woman in Athens with binoculars.

Your daughter, she's going with me.

Another way of saying she thinks she'll meet a tall dark and sensitive Latin.

You'll see. Travel's good for you. You need a change.

Another way of saying she'll drink too much one night and go to bed and wake in a fever and think she's going to die without ever having lived life to the hilt.

Miss Armstrong, there, through the green lily roots, fissures, to the stream in the rock, underground river. Ocean.

Another way of saying, Oh. I could have. I should have. Would that I.

The green salty enormous swarming sea . . . the dark-bottomed, wavy ocean.

Another way of saying oh.

You need make-up. I just thought of it. You need a new face. We can find colours. You need the neutral eye. Miss Armstrong. The neutral eye.

Keep jostling. Keep loving. Keep peace. Keep.

Hey look! Watch this. Gasoline on the water. Watch me press my face against the surface. There. How's that?

I was such a dreamy child. Once I spent a whole summer's day watching blue flax flowers waving in the breeze against the brick wall of our house, listening to bees fumbling in the great soft heads of the rhododendron blooms.

I'm going.

She won't follow you.

She might.

All right, go then. A heron is flying over. The evening heron.

She's following, Miss Armstrong. We may never come back.

Duck feet duck bellies duck beak dipping. Never. As if to say never. A man from Boston swimming far out in the Atlantic, no land in sight, he's wearing goggles, he sees the barnacled hull of his boat, tears fill the goggles, he relives a car crash, the death of his best friend's daughter. A squadron of flies hovers just above the surface, fish wait below, angling. Mr Armstrong my father bought a brand new car and a brand new television the same day. I remember the car, but my sister Bea remembers only the arrival of the television. He borrowed the money from God. He kept God's money in a separate compartment of his wallet. There is a very slight circular current to this lake. Bea is the spinster Armstrong. Alf James is a man's name. Natalie Wood's a movie star. Nadine you fell farther than I and I was a fallen woman. The dead can only remember the living. In God's world the hive can't leave the bees. A hive without a queen sounds different than a hive with a queen. I remember giving myself, I couldn't help it, I thought day and night how I would no longer be intact, I would belong to Alf, I'd be in love and have love, love would fill my heaven and I'd have heaven on earth. My soul was a dervish scurrying, chasing its tail in a smokescreen, a dust storm. His beard burning my chest, lips cooling. A hawk circles overhead, slower and slower, wider and

73

wider, scanning the glass of a tiny lake. He sees me, a mote in the brimming eye. Lousy fate and ordinary betrayal. But it was God's money I lent to Alf set me swimming from Bea's disappointment. A queenless roar. To think we were cheek to cheek at Christmas. We were the orphan Armstrongs, asking each other, How many years till a child's not a child, at what age does one become adult, when is a parent's death not cruel abandonment, will we give away a tenth of our inheritance, stay together? And answering I don't know, never, never, and yes, yes. No secrets. We will always tell each other everything, we will alternate cooking, smoke only one cigarette a day in the evening after supper, then read aloud, go to bed and get up early, walk by the lake at dawn, discuss our book, tell stories.

## 3. NADINE IN THE WORLD

A woman from the Marshall Islands is not yet dying of cancer, but has had many malignant tumours removed from inside her body; she was three when the American military executed their tests. An intelligent woman, she speaks well.

A nervous brown-haired woman with grey eyes lies in a Toronto hospital the second day of injections and testing: her third attempt at *in vitro* fertilization; the government health scheme won't help pay for the treatment next time. She's counting, whispering percentages: less than twelve last time, less than ten now? Half a pack of cigarettes. She's given up cigarettes; she's in hospital with no illness, with only desire for a child. She's not ill; she begins to feel weak.

In several basement studios in cities round the world several women are mock-raped by a mock-gang of mock-men. They are tied up and beaten, and utensils are used to enter them. A lot of money changes hands—they are tied up again and beaten again, and again utensils are used to enter them—there's incredible tension in the air—

A woman of an oppressed race and social class is being co-erced into surgery by officials with briefcases. Before she says, Okay, okay, got it, she's assured by a woman in a nice dress that her infertility will be temporary.

On the line in Sandra's yard hang towels and trousers and dresses in descending order, properly pegged. Inside, the fridge works perfectly, is stocked with food for the week in daily order. The cupboard ditto with supplies for the month. Whites already washed requiring ironing wait near the ironing board. By the sink frozen food on plates: apples for pie, meat for dinner. On the desk of her favourite room a box of coupons, scissors, last week's shopping flyers, reading glasses and a pen. Each bed has been made; the upstairs carpets bear vacuum cleaner grooves. A scarf slips from the bannister rail, lands by the dusty hall mirror.

Nadine and Judy swim out of the lake and go round the world and see everything there is to see and there is a lot because nothing is hidden. It all is just clear and plain, not like looking out a window, through binoculars, at a TV, through a windshield, not anything like that. Squeaky clean right in front of them so each can touch, put her fingers her mouth her tongue her kiss right up against it—and fresh when it's fresh and rotten when it's rotten. And it isn't good and evil, nothing like that, just things there, things, there. And going from one thing to the next and not counting but saying, Okay, okay, got it, and not making a list putting things in order, just recognizing, haunting, going on.

And so Nadine is dead, and the dead do not sing. Not horrible to be dead, to not sing. She has no worries, for instance, about how such a large all-consuming gesture has been interpreted—is being and will be interpreted, for death goes on and on. Death is not absolute except to the dead, and the dead show affection through silence.

Judy is profound silence, *carte blanche*, *tabula rasa*, in a sense reborn, for she passed from Miss Armstrong's still water to the lake's subtle currents and has known the world only through her mother's stories, which to her appeared as slight opacities in the general clarity, a sudden algae bloom that quickly vanished. A century ago she'd have sought her father, who would have bound her to him as property, but today she's triply useless: baby, girl, and dead. She's Miss Armstrong's paraphernalia, a trivial runaway. She can't haunt unless she imagines the world her mother's womb.

Nadine is not reborn, she remains dead, she travels and she witnesses and she is dead, and she's Nadine and she's dead. She learns more and more till she's learned everything, till were she alive she'd feel no more pain no more horror no more fear. She won't speak; Nadine who attends murders was woman and victim. She visits Clarence, who is one man, perhaps a victim too, a victim who tends victims. He played her murderer, he is guilty, and she is dead. He is a person, it was a person. She sees this. Nadine was a woman and Clarence is a man and he . . . attends and she attended. It was a person and Nadine.

Suppose she died for you, for us: she'd be killed again.

In cold blood. That's Clarence's cold blood, Patrick's creation. They don't understand so they figure it deeper, make it complicated. M is for mystery. Get that blood spot to talk. It's a daughter's blood talking to her mother, say that. Patrick and Clarence maybe feel a little dizzy but it will pass. Mr Travis is confused: What is happening? The blood says, Mama quick tell me what to do mama quick quick tell me before he comes!

A whole lake is too much, can't be imagined, but that's atrocity. METAPHOR. A fish out of water. SYMBOL. Mrs Travis. Redundant.

Mr Travis sends away for "the most important locomotives of all time in intricately handcrafted solid pewter."

Everybody is hungry. They want their dinner. They want their dinner. They want to have it tonight and every night. They want everybody else to have their own dinner and leave them alone. They will work hard all day to ensure that everybody has his own dinner. They will cross borders (hand over fist, tongue in cheek, stiff upper lip). Help their neighbours have dinner. They will forgive strangenesses like chopsticks, knife and fork. As long as at the end of the day they can have their dinner. They don't mind getting it themselves. They don't mind good service, a decent menu, a familiar smiling face. They will eat their fill and sleep all night long. They want nothing more, just dinner, and sleep.

In fact, Patrick does have something on Clarence (he really did see the launching of the body on the lake), and Clarence did, accidentally (he got carried away), murder Nadine. But during the production of Orff's musical they have many all-night discussions about passion, morality and death, and in an intense intellectual and finally non-physical way (to Clarence's disappointment), they fall madly in love. It need hardly be said that the superaddition of actual murder, death, and real criminality to their dialogue fuels some truly explosive and devastating dawn brandies.

Clarence he's a lucky man, a free man, hasn't even lost his wife. He trusted her, told her what he'd done, and Sandra came through. Patrick goes with Clarence and Sandra to Virginia. Clarence and Sandra go with Patrick to London. Judy shimmers convulsively.

Nadine she sees this, Nadine. Believes everything because no one tells her how to think, no one. No way to run a life but a good way to do what she does. What she does is she does death and there isn't a word for what you do when you do death, not a word in the English language. Menus are in French the language of love the language of male nouns, no help there. What she does isn't a noun of any gender, isn't a verb, isn't a pronoun. How she gets from place to place is she gets, how she sees what she sees is she sees, how she stops looking is she stops looking, how she gets somewhere else and looks at something else is she gets she looks. And when she's seen everything she's seen everything. She sees everything again, adjectives tone of voice everything everything.

In Arlington, Virginia, they walk round the burial ground of the nation's heroic dead and see the Tomb of the Unknown Soldier. They go to Washington's mother's home in Fredericksburg, and to Mount Vernon, Washington's country place. In Richmond, they visit Houdon's marble statue of Washington in Thomas Jefferson's Capitol, and the Edgar Allan Poe shrine.

In the British Library they all scan a book, *Children's Employment Commission, 1862*. In which it is given as:

Evidence: John Baker's, Bethnal Green (Match Maker).

Mary Ann Prancer (seems about 14) does not know how old she is. Lives in master's house and works partly as servant and partly in here at box making. Does that for her living and a shilling a week to clothe herself. Works here and in the house till about 10 o'clock.

Never was at school in her life. Does not know a letter. Never went to a church or chapel. Never heard of "England" or "London," or the "sea" or "ships." Never heard of God. Does not know what He does. Does not know whether it is better for her to be good or bad.

And of the children match makers: Their clothes shine in the dark, they cough, grow hoarse. Work at least 11 hours per day in confined areas.

Judy's unused to so much violence, so many monuments. She disintegrates and comes together each second, till the heart inside her ghost body is cluttered. She wobbles, but at the same time is delighted. Thirty years of space, and now there's launchers sending rockets every time she blinks.

The dam is completed, the river diverted, a twenty-year agreement to supply America with hydro-electric power ratified, and the lake by the village floods the adjacent valley. Bea Armstrong has to leave her father's house. All summer she avoids the huge lake. The other Miss Armstrong is now so thin that she occupies only the surface millimeter of water. Glynis Tilley climbs the fence one moonlit September night and is the first to swim the lake, the first swimmer to explore its new shores. As she glides through the warm soft black fluid, the last of Miss Armstrong evaporates, for a second steams above the girl's shoulders, and Glynis feels ecstatic, marvellous—a bubble of happiness sends her plunging under, holding her breath, counting strokes, one two three four five six—

Judy watches. Nadine reaches to cup a hand round the back of her fragile head.

Mr Travis builds the Rocky Mountains and sends the 1941 "Big Boy" over the top. Sandra bears a healthy baby girl.

# Chinese Ideas

I'm thinking it's as though we all ate something. It's a poison case, simple as that. The whole population sick and don't know it. No one was there; everybody was someplace else, as if that's an excuse, as if that excuse means we can't read a human soul by looking at a face or hearing a voice. I'm thinking our alibis are full of holes; we have swallowed murder and there is rape on our breath.

Maybe it's just the booze in my system.

I'm hung over and newly drunk at the same time.

These can't be tears.

It's booze coming out of my eyes. Been at it since Christmas. Something's got to give, crack in the dam and all.

I'm carrying my sister and I'm not cold. I'm thirteen, walking with my boyfriends, holding my baby sister who is asleep, hanging round my neck, but asleep, facing me, head on my shoulder, sleeping. And we're walking the dark road, in the headlights. I'm in the middle, a boy on each side. My sister weighs nothing at all; I could carry her forever. We're going slowly along, nobody speaking, the boys pushing their hands in their pockets, baby's head bumping my shoulder.

I feel sick, like dysentery, don't know what to do. No significance in these moments of family. Only goodbye or hello. Frozen memory. I'm forty-two. Should've at least had a baby. Baby like a desert to dry up these tears. But remembering my sister, Mom and Daddy, is like a nativity. Like one frame from a page of funnies. Some strip I read every day, so familiar it hurts.

It's almost noon. I take my whiskey and sit on the toilet. How long? How many times in a life does a person steam and push and think here it comes? Oh glory! When my stomach's quieter I will think more quietly.

How long have I been at odds with the world?

Always is the answer—no, that seems too recent. In case I throw up, the empty clay bowl rests on my knees, every chip in its rim reassuring. It belonged to my grandmother, who made her own bread. The bathroom's awash with sweat. I put my head in the bowl and feel the cool smooth bottom against one cheek. With dry lips I kiss the sides.

And I've stopped breathing. A while back everything smelled wrong.

I know nothing. I don't know from doors. Nothing from doors is nothing. Doors from nothing is doors. What I know.

I've stopped eating. Everything tastes of teeth. I've stopped eating. Driving, too. Let rust eat my sedan. A woman is dead— a stranger, so it shouldn't matter. Nadine. Don't remember when. Sometime last summer. Why is another question. The place I live is seedy, mould creeping up the walls, bits on the carpet. Wish I could stop hearing gears grind. I could afford better, no doubt. I could afford a nice bungalow in the suburbs, a carport for my car.

I'll have to try and get dressed and go to the mall. When I'm feeling really down I walk to Zellers and visit the budgies and canaries in their tiny cages. It's the last thing to do. Especially when I get my period and am too low for my own company. Half an hour standing in front of those birds way back of Zellers, under that white light, far from anything natural or homey, and I'm so truly broken-hearted that what I was before Zellers could be called carefree. Sometimes at Zellers I can forget my personal blues. I can feel kind of all right in a topsy turvy manner of feeling all right. We are such a sorry bunch, wandering the aisles.

Take my father.

My dad bases his life on Jonathan Livingston Seagull. He heard the tape about fifteen years ago when he was a factory worker and it blew his mind. Richard good-old-King-Arthur-in-Camelot-someone-left-the-cake-out-in-the-rain Harris on about flying. Meant nothing to me or my sister. But Dad's into really big real-estate deals now and he attributes his success to that tape. He shows consideration of others by smoking only with other smokers, only outside, giving people room to breathe; plus he always pays for everyone's time. When he visits me he leaves smoke-free air and a lot of dough, leaves me dizzy, coming and going in a whirl, a fan of notes on the table. And my expensive time goes on like the moon, sometimes fat, sometimes thin, but endless. I could buy a whole new life with each visit. He doesn't need to pay my sister because she's married to Kermit, King of the Chartered Accountants, but his second wife he pays, since they stopped living together. More and more he gives her, till she's become so rich that no one except him can get near. It's okay because I can't stand to be with her—she's that lonely.

If it were really possible to buy a life, I'd pass, thank you just the same. This one's already too much.

One Sunday last August, I met a man and two women at a party and gave them a ride to where the man said he lived. Clarence and Nadine and Sandra. The women didn't talk but Clarence was pretty drunk. He talked. He said one was his wife, one was a hooker. Wanted me to guess which was which. Tough choice, since Sandra was twice the age of Nadine. At his place they got out but Nadine got right back in. She said Clarence was an asshole and she wanted to return to the party. I said okay. Clarence kicked my car door and made a dent. Then he and Sandra went into the house. Nadine was in no shape. She didn't say anything. She just cried. I said I'd take her to my place. Not at first but eventually she said okay, but she had to get some stuff from the party. When we arrived there, I watched her cut through the bushes round back. The people in the windows of the house were dancing-drunk, screeching-drunk. I sat in my car maybe fifteen minutes. A beautiful summer dawn, light coming in the sky, sky full of little dark grey and white clouds, light starting in several places at once, some edges turning pink, a few drops of rain falling. Then I saw a man and a woman in the trees at the side of the house. It was Nadine—I recognized her dress—and she was with Clarence. He must have followed us. They were fighting hard, but not making any noise. They were battling under that boiling sky, in a garden so still the colours seemed to jump off what they belonged to. I called out, tried their names, but they wouldn't answer or stop fighting. I phoned the cops from the house. When I came outside again, they'd gone.

I read in the paper that out in the middle of China families are nailing daughters' bodies to their coffins to keep the souls from escaping.

Can you imagine this?

This has stayed in my head and I can't get it out. Like a door opening and inside is Christmas and Easter at the same time. Where in the dead bodies of young girls would they put the nails? Who would do the hammering? The girls were suicides, thinking to escape the narrow lives in store for them. Parents wanting to control their daughters to that extent gives me the shakes. And if it's not true, what kind of a person would make up such a story? What kind of a world would have newspapers to print these tales?

It took the police a short time to believe that Nadine wasn't murdered, that she committed suicide. It doesn't matter. None of it makes sense. It wouldn't prove anything one way or the other.

I am a heavy-drinking woman and recently in my heaviest-drinking moments I think about the country girls out there in the middle of China all dressed up to kill themselves believing they'll return and live like in a movie because they've travelled and they've seen cities where girls their own age are rich and free, and I believe it, I believe it.

During and right after the inquest I talked to everyone. I shot my mouth off about everything. I knew it was murder. I knew for sure. Probably rape, too. Oh yes, fresh sperm had been found in the body. I raved. I used up all the certainty of speech I knew. I woke up talking, went to sleep and dreamed conversations. They said I was a key witness. I wanted to nail that guy Clarence, and I wasn't going to mention China to anyone; they'd figure I was nuts. But when I talked to my sister on the phone and she said I shouldn't sound so angry in front of reporters, I spilled it about China, about the daughters there. She was quiet, then laughed. A fairy tale, she said, a modern folk myth.

I don't know. A folk myth? I said. A fairy tale?

Nadine and Sandra were both brunette and good looking. On the night in question Nadine wore a lot of make-up and a short pink dress, very tight. The drops of rain were so big they made dark splotches on her padded shoulders. She seemed so young. Sandra, I remember, was wearing a light blue shirt and baggy grey pants.

Cop eyes go hooded when you talk about women's clothes.

Clarence is about forty-five with long nails. His hands look soft. At the party he'd been wearing a black leather jacket and blue jeans, a gold chain round his neck. He was loud, drunk, stoned on coke, argumentative.

He wore a business suit at the inquest. Sandra had on a smart skirt and jacket ensemble. She said hardly a thing, looked like she'd been through the mill.

I talked to him at the party. Clarence. He hit on me. The reason I let him hit on me was because of the other women, the beautiful women he was with. He said things like, Your trust, your opportunity, your mission, your father, your mother, your future, your maturity, your frustration, your olive, your olive pit, your lips, your tongue, your guilt, your responsibility, your debt, your strength, your bravery, your isolation, your helplessness, your joy, your anxiety, your thing, your sophistication, your pleasure, your desire, your existence, your smell, your teeth, your impatience, your anger.

My role as witness in Nadine's death proves two things. That I can want to help someone (I'm thinking of Sandra), and that I want revenge. My sister says I'm muddle-headed and not fit to judge anyone. She is right. Like the police, she was certain that Clarence was innocent. Look at the evidence, she said.

At the inquest, my sister, the uncrowned Queen of Justice, sits at my father's right hand, her husband Kermit at his left. She's even got Dad and Kermit tolerating each other's clean air. This past Christmas my sister manoeuvred the whole family into festive gaiety. She baked shortbread and smiled and played with the kids and sang carols through it all. Father blessed the turkey, the tree, the pudding. I smoked and drank and emitted cool black waves. To Kermit's sainted children—a boy, a girl, well versed Christmas Eve by their grandfather in the attainments of Jonathan—I was invisible; they will be rich for sure.

Since Christmas I've stopped talking. No more nightlife. My father's visits are shorter and shorter, though he leaves more money each time.

Soon it will be spring.

In Zellers I listen to the canaries and find out who I am. In Zellers—all light, tough shine on the floors—the difference between the happy and the unhappy is hard to tell. Faces are smooth and getting smoother. My one eye that I can see in the stainless frame round the cages looks young. I have a young eye. It makes me think of my sister. My sister wears her perfect complexion like a caricature of my own; it masks her version of my fecklessness. We've always stood in front of Father like human beings, she in her sobriety, me in my drunkenness. At memories of our mother we both shy like spooked horses. With that one eye staring at itself I can hear the canaries fussing about, their claws snicking the perches, and hear the budgies warbling together against the booming of the ventilation system. I am hoping, no, praying, that some folk—ordinary people, not saints, not children—live in the world, live completely and innocently there.

Christmas was a farce, and yet beneath the surface was a kind of glowy heat. I didn't notice it at the time, but it comes to me now. Like coals raked over the morning after a big fire. In movies of close families I never want anyone to die. Sometimes to go on thinking is to go on thinking about people, and that's out for me. If I had nerve, to be with people who seemed lovely would be okay. I cry through a whole movie if someone dies. No one can see me. No one sees me now. In Zellers everyone shines in a fever! Tragic families dream deep dreams as they stop and start through the departments. They could be walking the dark sleeping prairie. They could be asleep in bed. Now I want only to drink. I want to drink up all hard surfaces, cars, men, the world and other women; it is avarice. I am as chicken as anyone who ever lived. Men over at the counters ask politely for money.

In the end, of course, I have a home. Got three homes to go to: my father's my sister's my own. I am so happy. See my family. My family, my home. I guess everyone has a lousy self-image.

This morning I was sick with the vision of carrying my sister, and all day I've been thinking of Nadine and the Chinese suicides. This afternoon, though, in Pet Supplies at Zellers, I feel better. Still weak and dizzy, but better. If my sister ever had some problem and came to me with it, I'd bring her here. I'd say something like, Sweetheart, these poor shoppers have nowhere left to go; and these birds can sing even here. Inside every person is a cage, and in every cage is the idea of love.

# Chaste

Sometimes you think there's not enough time, or no time to spare. Then there's too much time; you don't know what to do with it. Here I am, at the end of summer. The sprinklers, the crowd, the trees.

"Dad's never disappeared like this before," says my daughter. She's such a worrier. Although I agree with her that it's probably a good idea to keep leaving messages wherever we go—Glendale, Bishop Cridge, the hospital—I don't think we're justified in taking taxicabs. The rental bus carrying the rest of the singers is not really slow, never more than half an hour late. I don't understand her panic to arrive everywhere exactly on time.

My husband was supposed to drive us, but he's vanished into thin air. Gets me mad, Helen's fretting, does no good. He'll show up soon now I'm sure. He knows our itinerary. If Helen would only shut up I could think. I'd remember something he said to me, some plan of his, some clue. Perhaps he had a headache and has gone back to Helen and Alex's. Helen treats the cabbie like an untrustworthy servant, the same way she treated the nurses and orderlies. I expect she's picked up the habit from

Alex. He was born into that world of servants, if that's an excuse, but she wasn't. When I think of telling her off I don't know where to begin.

We sang a lot of hymns at the hospital—they wanted hymns, not show tunes—but I've still got *Good Night, Irene* going round in my head. Good night, Irene, good night, Irene—

"What's that, Mother?"

"Nothing. Just mumbling."

Somewhere there's a quiet place with a comfy chair and he's there, looking up in mild surprise at all the fuss, ready to explain why he disappeared. Soon Helen and I and her choir will sing the last of the songs, and we'll be able to go home, meaning to Helen's big fancy house. It's inevitable.

Well, my husband has not materialized. So I swim lengths and lengths of the family pool beside the tennis court. I've always been a strong swimmer. A long time ago I was the first person to swim round the home lake in December. I said I'd do it and I did. I have a newspaper clipping to prove it. Glynis Tilley was my name before I married. Now it's Glynis Arnason. I said I'd stay always with my husband, and I have. Forty-three years.

My grandson Greg Martinet is twelve years old, big for his age, and his father is teaching him to drive. The lesson was planned a week ago and Alex thinks it best to pretend nothing is wrong, at least for today. Helen and I look on from the veranda. We've just called the police. My skin smells of chlorine. We're drinking brandy. Helen's face turns toward me slow as an owl's and I'm lying again by Piet's side, upstairs in bed, listening with every nerve.

"Mom, are you all right?"

"Why must Alex teach Greg to drive—he's too young. He looks terrified."

Helen sips from her big round glass. "Alex learned when he was that age. Greg's scared of everything. If he learns how simple it is to drive a car . . . "

We stand together at the veranda railing. I want to be friends, want to talk of how parents can be wrong about their children.

Ordinary conversation seems impossible now with Piet gone, pointless. There's been a family accident and I've been thrown clear. I feel calm and as transparent as this beautiful snifter, completely strong. But I've no warmth to spare. I close my eyes and see Piet walking up the driveway toward the house. He's young again. He's carrying a suitcase. He'll want to make love because he's been away, and I don't want to make love, not when I feel so perfect—but now, seeing Piet, I feel guilty, almost as though I've been unfaithful—

Greg releases the clutch too fast; the car stalls. He looks defeated. Alex, stiff as a board in the passenger seat, shrugs in our direction. They're like a comedy team in this odd warm light.

"Of course Greg is too young," says Helen. "I've never been sure about pushing him like this. Alex is sure though. And Greg does seem more confident."

After a late supper, I'm weary of Helen's *what ifs* and Alex's *don't let's jump to conclusions*, and I'm finding it difficult to concentrate. "I'm tired. I'm going to bed," I tell them. "You can stay by the telephone and worry, if you like."

"I'm sure everything's fine, Mom," says Alex.

Upstairs I peep at my sleeping girl, my grandaughter, cross the hall to Piet's and my room, undress and crawl under the covers. I read for a few minutes, then lie on my side in bed and watch through my door the black space of Sheila's upper doorway. Listen! She's breathing; so'm I. I should be worried sick, but I'm not. At this moment I experience loss the way a five-year-old would: I don't believe in it.

"It is not always easy to tell the difference between thinking and looking out of the window." That's a line I read in Wallace Stevens's letters. It tickles me. Does Alex always practice this late? I hear the bounce of a tennis ball between board and racquet. Whack. Experience. Ping. Loss. Thud. At any moment it's possible for any child to love any person. You just have to provide the right situation, the right ingredients. I've had lots of experiences, many losses. Alex has had lights installed round the court. He had to show them off first thing when we arrived. Ripples from the pool cross my ceiling. Every so often the curtain blows right into the room; now and then the ball hits the wire fence. I'm sleepy. Piet, where are you? Tennis angels above me lock fingers in the mesh. My dear. A flock of gulls crying overhead. Late for birds, too.

"Can I have a glass of water?" Sheila wakes us all in the middle of the night. Alex Martinet, my son-in-law, stands in my bedroom doorway in his underwear.

"What we need," he says, "is a good detective. A *good* detective, yes, and to get hold of any friends of Piet's who might be living in the area. Any that Mom's not thought of. Maybe a business acquaintance?"

"What has become of him?" Helen enters to say. She's actually wringing her hands. "People can't vanish. He couldn't have run away. I mean he couldn't, could he? Mom?"

"He's not a teenager," I tell the silhouettes. "He's firm of mind, steady of purpose. But maybe yes. Perhaps that's just what he's done." "But aren't you worried?" Helen asks.

"I want Grampa. I want Grampa."

"Sheely, go to sleep," says Alex. "You'll see him soon, I promise." They both take a step into my room. "Helen's right, you must be worried. Maybe we all should take a sleeping pill. I know I haven't slept a wink. Tomorrow we'll get organized. Okay, Helen? Okay, Mom?"

"Okay."

"Are you crying?" says Helen.

"No."

"You are. Alex, she's crying." And Helen begins to sob. There in my bedroom in the dark my daughter is crying in her husband's arms.

"I'm fine," I say. "Fine. Now go on back to bed, you two."

"I feel so helpless," says Helen. "What can we do, Alex?"

"We probably know something, one of us probably knows something that would prove helpful, but it's not easy to put it all together. We're nervous and overtired, we have suspicions—"

"This nonsense is not helping anyone." I have to stop him. Helen's snuffling is getting worse. "I'm quite able to sleep. I don't want a pill. Good night."

Of course! What we need is a good detective. A *good* detective, yes, and to get to the bottom of this. Alex will make everybody tell when they last saw Piet, what their last conversation with him was about. Did he seem upset? Was he acting strange? He will add it all up, no doubt. It's an interesting puzzle. Piet. Where are you, dear? I know you're not dead, not hurt. What has this to do with me? What does it mean? Is there anything of you that is not of us? We're almost the same person. Listen to that wind. I know something, but it's not clear what I know. Except it's not a trick. You're a simple man, not capable of trickery. Are you capable of abnormal behaviour? We made love again, after years of abstinence, in this very bed. Should I tell Alex and Helen? Is it significant? They'll think it alarming, or think there's another woman. They'll trot out theories like crooks inventing alibis. "Where were you the day grampa disappeared?" They'll assemble a mountain of facts, a brigade of detectives, diviners—and I'm falling asleep, g'night love.

It's Interrogation Monday, and we've been grilled, and what we've learned amounts to this: All Saturday we ate the same food, shared the same water; kids were splashing in the pool, our kids, our kids' kids. It was our annual Labour Day weekend reunion. We spent no money; we ate outside; it felt like our moment. Everyone agrees we had a wonderful time. They think they can speak for Grandad. Alex remembers you saying, "It's a real shame it couldn't last all year." Isn't that silly, but you know it sounds like something you would say. What I can't stop thinking, what it comes down to, what we shouldn't forget is we *were* pretty happy. So how could what happened have happened? How does anything happen? Has anything happened?

We drove down for the long weekend, arrived Friday night, were to have returned Tuesday, tomorrow, after walking Sheila to her first day at kindergarten, after seeing Greg off on the bus to his boarding school. You know all this as well as I. What you don't know is the wind has left the pool scattered with bright rowan berries and first autumn leaves. Friday and Saturday nights we made love—for slow hours it felt like—in the dark, in the mild September bug-free air from the open window. You know this, too. We could smell the sea as we fell asleep. And it was delicious, both nights. I've never felt closer to anyone in my life. I wouldn't want to go back in time, wouldn't go back over the years we've spent together. No, as lovely as they often were, I wouldn't go back to those times. But I will return to these past nights in our daughter's house. The big house, the big bed groaning the first, the second night; then last night, me alone on my back in the middle of the bed, feet and hands at each corner, for four hours of dreamless sleep, a melodramatic intermission, and four more hours of dreamless sleep. The breeze kept me cool, and I didn't budge an inch till morning.

The starlings are still busy in your singing tree. This morning I walked the same route we walked Sunday morning, before we were to help Helen do her "Charity Rondelet" as you put it. The same dabchick families strutted the same mudflats down to the water. But I didn't recognize anywhere the silent tree. There are too many quiet trees.

Friday night we dropped to sleep immediately after making love. Saturday, however, we stayed awake a while. We talked over the day, how nice it had been, talked of how acquisitive our daughter had become.

"Alex is a prominent citizen," you said.

"Yes, he is. Is and ever will be."

"They seem afraid, somehow," you said.

"We're not afraid, are we?"

"No."

"Do you understand me if I say I feel so good?"

"I feel quiet," you said. "It's late. Did you hear the owl?"

"Yes."

"He stopped when we did?"

"*She* stopped."

"*She* stopped."

"I'm drifting, love, going to sleep now."

"I wonder why we're not afraid," you said. "D'you think it's because we're old? And no need for us to ask, about this, what happened, is there? No need for us to ask what was that, what did you want, what did I, what did we do. In effect nothing has changed. But . . . "

"Sleep, Piet, sleep."

You were right, Alex is, no, *both* are afraid. Helen and Alex only think they're concerned about your disappearance. In fact it gives them something to focus their fear on. It's another convenient mystery. I heard Alex on the phone this morning tell his tennis partner they wouldn't be able to play today because his father-in-law is missing. The big phony deep voice. And Helen, red-eyed, eating nothing at breakfast. Shushing the kids. They can't help it, but they're enjoying themselves. I must find a way to say stop. What we need is not a good detective. Everybody told their story. Each member of the family has told their story and the facts have been added up. We don't need the police. It seems to me they want murder or something awful to have happened. Helen says it's her way of dealing with the world. She must think the worst, she says. She has to imagine every possible scenario.

"*Scenario?*" I said.

"Mother," Helen warned.

"Come on you two," said Alex. "I'm trying to talk to an operator."

"How can you cope with anything without eating?" I whispered. "That's right, Mother, I'm not hungry. It's a normal physiological reaction to shock."

But it's sinister, Helen not eating while I'm ravenous. And the way they all watch me. As if Helen and Alex and even the kids want me to swallow dreadful possibilities. Piet Arnason, why couldn't you have disappeared at home?

The train whistle. When did I notice it before? Clouds have rolled across the sky this afternoon. We heard some thunder earlier and now it's raining. I find it difficult to place events in any kind of order. Yesterday time started growing and it hasn't stopped. You were to drive the car into town and meet us in the flower shop at The Bay. The kids are swimming in the rain, while Helen and Alex and I stay by the phone. I wonder if it's raining back home. It will keep the dust down, will wash the leaves. Alex has the phone to his ear a lot of the time. He's calling Alberta, calling the Kootenays, calling Vancouver. Between calls he folds his arms and waits. The train whistle. The train whistle. It's stuffy in here, even with the window open. It *isn't* easy to tell the difference between thinking and staring out. Rain hisses on the surface of the pool. Helen wears a shawl and has situated herself behind the curtain so she can shoot glances at Sheila and Greg who look like they're doing water ballet. What about that horn? *Sweetheart, sweetheart*, what I wanted to remember, the train whistle. I did dream. I dreamed of you as an ape man: you were crazy, crying like a saxophone. You thought you'd lost me, but I was with you. We were in the jungle. You were looking for me everywhere, but my body was glued to your furry back as you ran and ran.

So here we are after dark at the post-modern kitchen table drinking single malt scotch. I won't let them pull the blinds and turn on the fluorescents. Greg and Sheila watch TV in the next room. Weird lights flash beneath the kitchen door. Marsh gas. I want to go home.

"But we know he's not gone home," says Alex. "The police have checked your house more than once."

"I can't bear to think of you driving alone," says Helen. "If you must go back—and I think it's crazy—if you must go, then I'll come with you."

"We're doing everything we can," says Alex. "All our contacts have this number. It's just a matter of time. Someone will turn up something."

"Maybe you don't *feel* upset," says Helen. "But I know you well enough to know you're suppressing it. At home you'll have some kind of delayed reaction. You know you will. You'll get sick, then I'll have to come look after you."

"And," says Alex. "I don't want to be bleak, but we must be realistic. If something, well, if something unfortunate has happened, well I don't know, let's just assume—I mean I wouldn't be able to tell you over the phone, if you were—You'd want to be with your own—Of course if you're dead set on leaving us—"

"Can't you see it would be selfish, Mom?" says Helen.

"Oh, I don't think we can use words like that here," says Alex.

"Won't you at least say why it is you want to go home?" Helen asks. "Is it me?"

"We can give you Greg's room tomorrow," says Alex. "You'll have all the privacy you want."

"Shut up a sec and let her answer, Alex," says Helen. "Is it me? You can't stand being around me?"

"Helen," says Alex.

"Just be quiet," says Helen. "This is between Mom and me. You don't know anything about this."

"Maybe I should leave the room," says Alex.

"Good idea," says Helen.

There's the sound of gunfire from the TV room. I'm hungry again. Alex refills our glasses. Rain has squashed the huge-headed begonias that circle the pool.

"It's you I'm thinking of," says Helen. "You and Dad."

"Turn down that racket!" Alex yells. "We're trying to talk in here!" He stands up, sits again. "Listen," he says, "if you ladies would feel better alone here, I mean if I'm in the way, just say the word. I only want to help. I just thought I was easing the load, you know, taking care of the phone calls and so on, the investigation. I figured you wouldn't have to do a thing. Maybe I was wrong. Maybe you need to feel you're actively looking for Piet. Is that right, Mom? If I'm in the way, you know, taking over, say the word. I'll steer clear. I've lots of work at the office. I don't need to spend time doing this. It's just I'm concerned, Mom, I really am. It's so damned strange and all. What I say, then, is stay with us. Let us know what you want us to do—"

"Please, Alex," says Helen. "That's very nice, but you're repeating yourself. We appreciate what you're doing. Honestly.

But honey, I think Mom and I really need to talk." "I'll leave you two, then," says Alex. "Think about what I said. Let me know. I'm concerned. I'm just as concerned about you, Mom, as I am about Piet," he says. "I love you guys," he says. He stands up and opens the kitchen door. A lot of trebly TV voices are talking at once.

"Dad?" asks Greg. "What's a chastity belt?"

"What're you watching in here?" Alex says. He crosses the room and puts himself between us and the screen.

Helen says, "Mom, we've got to talk about you and Dad." She says, "There's something you're not telling me, isn't there?"

"What's chastity?" says Sheila.

"Go clean your teeth and put on your PJs," says Alex, switching off the set. "If you're in bed fast I'll tell you a dragon story. Away you go." He says to Greg, "No wisecracks out of you. Go get your packing finished."

Alex comes back to the kitchen and sits down again.

"Christ," says Helen. "Christ Christ Christ—"

The phone rings. Alex picks it up. "Hello? This is Martinet speaking. Yes? Arnason, right. The son-in-law. Yes, she's here. She's right here, but . . . One moment . . . It's the Nanaimo police, Mom. I can handle it if you want."

I shake my head, reach for the phone. They think I won't be able to speak.

"Yes?" I say. Helen mouths *Nanaimo?* at Alex, who puts his arm round her and holds tight. Suddenly she looks eleven years old and my eyes feel hot. Nanaimo, I'm thinking, what a strange word. Nanaimo. And it's a hundred miles away. Not jungle, but rain forest.

A body has been found, it seems, the body of a man answering the description of my husband. They want to know about the gold ring.

"Yes," I say.

And a birthmark.

"Yes," I say. A badly scarred right forefinger.

"Yes," I say.

The faces of my daughter and her husband loom across the table, full of worry. I don't know what my face is doing. Sheila arrives in the doorway, fresh and clean, each hand clutching a sheet of paper with a drawing. The man at the other end of the line is saying appropriately sad things. He explains that foul play is not suspected. He says it was likely a heart attack and a fall, or a fall and a heart attack. Finally, he asks would I be able to go to Nanaimo tomorrow, would tomorrow be all right for the official identification. Helen looks white and stricken. I want to take her in my arms. As I hang up, Alex is hustling Sheila from the room.

"Alex, wait," I say. "She wants to show me something."

"It's Grampa," Sheila says, scrambling to my side. She holds up the faces she has drawn and coloured. The faces smile. Sheila is smiling. She smells of soap and toothpaste. And she has done your eyes just right.

# The Day It Snowed on Maurice

Faye had first liked him because he reminded her of Uncle Frank. She remembered that. Though his name was William she called him Buzz. And that was because Uncle Frank once upon a time kept bees. What surprised her now was that she couldn't recall what Uncle Frank looked like or why she had loved him; William's image always got in the way. She'd not talked to anyone about Uncle Frank for years. Jill was too young to remember him and Faye had not spoken or written to Maggie for ages, and everyone else was dead. She'd not even tried to tell William about Uncle Frank. And therefore no one would know, even if they heard her use the name, why she called William Buzz. Of course no one in the office had ever heard her call him anything but William. It was important that their relationship be hidden from co-workers. But what was she think-ing of? It didn't matter any more what Uncle Frank had been like or what was meant by a cute nickname because William was gone; long ago Uncle Frank had gone, and now William was gone, and somehow everything was okay anyway.

Yesterday, the wrecked cottage had been an awful shock. She'd seen in it a glimpse of their coming week together. All would be crazy—stormy sex followed by stormy fights, fits of weeping, jealous spats, and sleepy drunken tenderness. But weird, Buzz's behaviour—almost a kind of wingy celebration—when confronted with the damage. It had to be some deep trouble that caused his first "ah well" reaction, then made him lose it the way he did, then made him disappear. She'd hoped, but figured (and now knew) otherwise, that she was on his mind. You cannot catch a person all the way through, was what she decided as she watched the tawny buck dance-stop-dance across the clearing. A tango, for some reason; bars of sunshine across the steamy grass of his path.

∞

"We're running against racism!"
  "Yes we are!"
  "We're running against famine!"
  "Yes we are!"
  "We're running against war!"
  "Yes we are!"
The children break from the forest into the clearing and onto the side of the Autobahn. Stuttgart children, unsponsored and breathless, hair flying in that still moment before dawn. Crows spooked, motorists amazed. The sun just beginning to nudge the horizon. The day of the world run will be glorious, televised or not, come rain or shine. Elsewhere in other dawns similar children are dashing along similar roads; earlier dawns spawned other kids, and some children are still asleep who in later dawns will also begin to run. Where it is very cold, where it is very hot. In cities and through jungles, along beaches, up mountains, across prairies.

∞

Proclivity.
  Marty listened to the word, felt a sourness in his belly. His brother had chosen the word, as he chose all words, care-

lessly. William was trying to be likeable, to seem liberal and hip and clever.

True, meeting the young man called Andrew for the first time, Marty had felt attracted, but he was not ready to recognize the erotic flavour, the particular tone, of the attraction. He wanted time to mull over this new presence. The months he'd be away would provide sufficient distance for cool appraisal, perhaps fueled by some occasional correspondence—a postcard, a letter or two. My dear Andrew. Dear Martin. He didn't approve of his brother's supercilious gut reaction. He'd always hated this in William, the way his brother, older than Marty by five years and a professor of economics, had to crudely analyse spontaneously and aloud to anyone who would listen a person's—especially Marty's—status *vis-à-vis* every other person.

Marty cleared his throat and looked at William's wife. She smiled at him; he smiled back. As always, she seemed a little fuzzy. He blinked. It was perhaps the way she wore her hair, sort of floating in blonde wisps away from her face. William was lumbering about the room, burning energy, sniffing out something else Marty might need on his trip, seeking other things to pack or put in order. Marty had the usual feeling of wanting to introduce them to each other; they resembled cheerful teddy bears who had yet to meet.

William was pouring new drinks. He had his jacket off and his sleeves rolled up. His collar showed grey and there were vague yellow stains under the arms.

"No, but seriously, Mart," he said, "Andrew is a great kid. He likes you. This new job of yours won't last forever. I think you should cement the relationship before you go away. Annette tells me you haven't even called him. She says he's obviously waiting for you to call. He's pining. Isn't that so, sugar?"

Annette turned her toothy grin in William's direction.

"He honestly does like you, Marty," she said. "I've sounded him out—indirectly, of course. He admires you enormously and he's such a sincere chap. And sensitive. I hate to see him involved in that fickle gay set at the university. It's dangerous for him. He'd like something steady, I just know he would. He's beautiful, so athletic. And he's not as young as he looks, you know." She sipped her drink. "You two looked handsome together playing tennis."

"For God's sake," said Marty. He turned to the window and watched the rain filling the great pools on the roof below. Andrew *was* beautiful. Something about him—perhaps his ears?—reminded Marty of Father Dmitri and of summer days in the cool basement of the dormitory building. When he was a young man, he and Father Dmitri had composed sonnets together on such unseasonably gloomy afternoons.

Annette and William avoided looking at each other. They were fidgeting among the boxes and piles of stuff yet to be packed as if to regret coming, regret drinking so much, staying so late. They looked fiercely independent and tired and he felt sorry for them, sorry for himself. They'd had two full days of driving to get here and had the return journey ahead. Marty's UN appointment had come through suddenly and the visit had been a farewell of sorts: very soon he would fly to Ottawa for briefing, then on to New York, then the Western Sahara; all evening he had felt stunned, nostalgic; now he felt himself becoming maudlin. They'd gotten quickly drunk, and were on the verge of saying stupid things. Marty kept thinking of Annette and William's two wonderful children; then he thought of Faye, William's latest mistress, of whom he was supposed to be ignorant. And with that thought, he deemed it essential they say good night.

"This place is a catastrophe," said William.

"Never mind," said Marty. "We should get some sleep. Tomorrow we'll put our backs to it. And thanks, you two. I do appreciate you rallying."

Annette sat down on a trunk and put her face in her hands. Horrified, Marty watched tears trickle between the fingers.

Just before going to bed, while Annette did whatever women did in bathrooms prior to sleep, William put his hand on Marty's shoulder. He confided to his brother that whenever he and Annette visited her mother he fell in love with a studio photographic portrait of his wife at eighteen.

Marty wanted to remove the hand. Embarrassed, he started to sweat as William pushed the scratchy fabric of the shirt about on his shoulder and described the length and lustre of Annette's hair. Her soft adolescent cheeks. The gold-framed photo stood, surrounded by plastic flowers, on the mantel of his mother-in-law's fireplace.

"It is like a fenestella, Mart," he said. "Ah, you know. I always feel I should wash my hands before that image. It's uncanny. There should be a piscina, a credence."

His fingers went on and on, pinching the wool, Marty's skin, digging deep for bone. Marty, through his exhaustion, through his disgust at this familiarity, this obtuse deception, heard William say in hushed tones that his love for the girl in the picture was growing steadily. Heard him say his mother-in-law reminded him of the boys' nanny of thirty years ago.

"Remember Miss Jane, Mart. That smile—"

"Good night, William," said Marty. "It's no use. I can't follow you any more. It's been a long day."

∞

"There's my mattress," said William. "And here's my mistress. I've not seen my mattress since the bed was last changed, since last year, last holiday. And now it's shredded. I've not seen my mistress since Tuesday. Look at that once-fine mattress. You can see the salesman was telling the truth: the springs, the construction, the whole assembly is as he promised. I had hoped to sleep with you, Faye, on that splendid mattress. I had hoped to dream. I had hoped to store nuts beneath."

Faye looked from William's beaming face to the slashed mattress, then let her gaze continue round the cabin.

All was a mess, all. Vandals had smashed nearly every breakable thing. The door hung from its hinges and yellow leaves drifted in. Soon it would be dark, and the rain would keep falling as it had fallen all last night as they tossed and groaned in the tent, as it had fallen all day on the drive here. When Faye began to pick things up, William lifted an intact plate, arced it over his head, brought the plate down hard on the table edge. He was grinning, grinning like a chimpanzee. Faye swept sharp fragments onto newspaper, emptied the paper into a bucket full of glass. She felt like stepping out in the rain, leaving this strange William to his chaotic cottage, and driving all the way home.

"Buzz," she said, "this is so sad."

"You know what I'm thinking, Faye-sugar?" said William. "I'm thinking of the first girl I loved. Her name was Boxy. I've been thinking about Boxy all day. She's married for the third time now, to this guy who works for a company that manufactures elevators."

∞

"Yes we are!"

"Yes we are!"

"Yes we are!"

Brisbane kids. Songhai kids. Sierra Leone kids. Dunkerque kids. Walloon kids. Lebanese kids. Setubal kids. Culpeper kids. When the sun wails too high and hot in the sky, when their fingers and toes are numb from cold, when rain washes out the road ahead, when wind whirls and their eyes catch fists of red dust, when sand scorches even fleeting feet, when snow and hail chime crystal on soft hair over eardrums—then the first marquees appear, and high-ranking soldiers welcome and attend the young runners with milk and honey ambrosia. Down on their knees, generals wash and salve the runners' feet. All the world's tents fill with the sweet scent of honeycomb, fresh cream, the sound of one breath breathing.

∞

Annette was on the telephone to Marty, pouring her soul into the mouthpiece. She imagined it strained, her soul, filtered through the tiny holes, arriving in Marty's ear pure and incoherent. This was the second time in an hour she'd called to tell him what he already knew. He'd known, he told on the first call, because one night by accident several months ago he'd seen Faye and William together. "What can I do, Martin? What can I do?" This call she was making from a truckers' cafe while William dozed in their room in the adjacent motel. Several months! The words she used to convey her pain to Marty were stale and melodramatic, as though she were telling a stranger the boring details of a tedious event. How she needed his wisdom on this matter! Tomorrow would be too late! She'd be home and therefore less desperate, and Marty would have flown to his briefing, and William would be packing for his secret sojourn at the cottage. "It must be terrible," Marty said, "to be in your shoes." Oh, she felt so small and vulnerable away from her house, away from the children who might be dead or maimed or spirited away. "I wish I'd managed to see you alone," she whispered to the phone. She heard Marty clearing his throat. "Yes," he said, "well, I wish I could say something helpful."

∞

While Faye was in the village supermarket, William wandered away from the truck. He bought clip-on sunglasses from the drug store, then strolled next door to the bus station where a Greyhound was idling. He bought a ticket to a place he'd never heard of, and boarded; as the vehicle juddered down the main street he saw Faye pushing a cart across the parking lot toward the truck, her head turning this way and that, not once considering the bus.

He waved at her through the tinted glass, but she didn't see him.

The man in the next seat was asleep; his shirt gaped to reveal a tattoo above his right nipple: *Maurice*.

∞

At that instant, Marty was feeling very awkward indeed as Andrew skillfully plied his little sports car through the heavy airport traffic. Andrew had turned up unannounced and had insisted on ferrying Marty to the terminal to see him off. Marty could not stop flustering internally about William and Annette. His brain felt cobwebby and feverish. And now Andrew, he felt sure, was on the verge of some clammy declaration. Something probably open-ended and honest, but requiring kindly response, sensitive reaction, an intelligent noncommittal murmur. Marty didn't think he was ready for any of these intrigues, any of these people who felt they must foist themselves upon others because they believed that that was what gave spice to life. Hot and moist and too close in the car. Small relationships unfurled rapidly and unpredictably enough; one should feel no compunction to actively seek a means to precipitate them.

"Did my brother put you up to this?"

"Up to what?" Andrew shifted gears. Marty watched the tendons writhe above the knuckles of Andrew's slim hand. "You know. Did he ask you to take me to the airport? Or was it Annette?"

"Oh, no. My idea." Andrew smiled a coy but charming smile. "I had to see you before you disappeared for such a long time."

"I could be back in a few weeks. One never knows with these things."

"No," Andrew echoed, "one never knows."

∞

Bird song ceases at noon, and the mile after mile of children effortlessly running along roads cleared of traffic beneath the amber light of early afternoon continues. Their rhythmic footfalls are accompanied by only deepening silence. Their own. Their own. Their own.

∞

Faye loaded the groceries carefully into the box behind the truck's cab; she remembered William saying that to avoid Annette he'd spent nearly the whole summer in his basement fixing that box. A very warm day, the pavement wobbling; in late September anything was possible.

Buzz was not in the liquor store, not in the tackle and video shop, not in the pharmacy. She pulled the keys from the ignition and stood a while in the sun, feeling sweat trickle from each armpit. People came and went but no one seemed to notice her. She didn't know why she wasn't angry. If he'd decided to walk back to the cabin, she'd catch him on the road. She thought again of disappearing, driving away. Several times last night she'd woken and known exactly, but not liked, where she was. Listening to Buzz snoring, she'd imagined getting up from their makeshift bed on the floor, stuffing her things into the overnight bag, and taking a powder. The darkness had seemed to last forever, with scurrying sounds from inside the walls, water dripping from the eaves. And thinking about the garbage round her and all the talking they'd have to do didn't help. You heard of people disappearing; people ran, vanished, built new lives for themselves. How was that possible?

"Buzz, you asshole," she said gaily as she reached the cabin and saw movement through the bedroom window.

∞

Annette went down to her garden where the children were playing and the dahlias were a picture. A white goose feathered itself into the pond surface. Across the valley sounded the rumble of heavy equipment gouging the hillside, widening the already too-wide highway. She put her hands on her hips. Cowbirds chuckled from the forest edge. The rose arbour. The rose arbour. Behind her waited the cool empty house, glass shelves, pot-pourri, room after room, darker and colder, till the last room, the north bedroom, darkest and coldest of all, summer sanctuary, where she would go to sleep this night, where she'd wake tomorrow morning, as she had woken this. Page by page, one of the beef cows in the neighbouring pasture was eating a paperback book; her pink tongue turned then tore each printed leaf from the book's spine. A thick book, swollen even thicker by last night's rain. Annette remained, arms akimbo, on the short grass beside the pond, listening to the highway crew, as half aware of her children's quiet game as they were of her near presence. How I am unpretty and no longer young, she thought. How this place is so beautiful, even the termites flying, the swallows hunting. As she'd done for fifteen years when William was away, she worked too hard—in the house, in the garden—then suddenly stopped like this, and did nothing. Somewhere during that period the children had arrived. Though she'd twice given birth, the children seemed to have always been there, part of her. How long had she been standing, just standing, in this position? The children didn't find her odd. Nor did the still goose in the dead centre of the water. The cow was having trouble with the last pages—the book kept sliding around on the grass. So once again Marty would be flying away, leaving the country, going to help others. She and William would see him in two days. They'd help him pack, and she'd try to approach the conversation she wanted to have with him—could only have with Marty because he was William's brother—a conversation she'd been rehearsing for a month, since discovering Faye's queerly devotional little notes to her husband. Soon she would go inside to her desk by the open french doors and she'd write her own brief business-like letters. Yes, and she'd sign cheques that might bring some measure of relief to the terribly deprived and hungry of the world. If her life was hopeless, let the world not be. But oh those brown huge eyes! What a lot of words to eat! And what a lovely September day it was, not too hot.

∞

Because she'd not talked to Maggie for such a long time, to phone now would be difficult. They'd have catching up to do, all kinds of chat to get through before she could say what she wanted to say. Then what she'd say would seem bizarre. But she had to talk to someone, and wasn't it bizarre what was happening to her?

The cabin was full of afternoon sun. It stank of wild animal. As she looked round, her skin crawled with gooseflesh. When she'd got to the door, tongue clicking in reprisal, not Buzz, but a huge buck deer, head high, antlers pricking the air, had stepped cool as ice from the inside dark to shoulder past her. He'd been close enough to touch. His eyes had looked into hers. His breath had been loud. She could still see him out there foraging, and if she closed her eyes his rack filled her consciousness. She had the notion she could feel its points pushing into ideas she'd never noticed before.

Jill, then. She'd seen Jill only last week. But Jill had never seemed a person to go to for help in any but the most ordinary hardship. And this was about as far from ordinary as you could get. She couldn't think of telling anyone but Maggie. Maggie would be the one for this kind of adventure. Maggie would know what to do. On the other hand, shouldn't she keep her thoughts where they belonged and simply quit the people she'd known the way they had surely (they had, surely, hadn't they?), as they surely had quit her? Hadn't she been abandoned more than once?

That was the main amazing thing of all the amazing things in this whole business: she could give up her job, close her bank account, and go where no one knew her. It could be that simple. For the first time she realized that she could vanish, and she could vanish without William, without anyone. She could, easy as writing and speaking, pay her bills, cancel her deliveries, and in a couple of phone calls tell everyone who knew her that she was happy and free and they should feel glad for her even though they'd never set eyes on her again. Finally she could admit to herself that she'd begun these escape plans in her head long ago, but always with a partner, latterly Buzz, alongside each thought. And now as this fresh new air blew through her, the notion of Buzz reappearing in the doorway waving a bottle of champagne or some other flashy extravagance as excuse for his absence sent her into a panic. She looked once at the phone, then quickly sorted her clothes from the debris. She would go without a word to anyone, not even her sisters, though she'd keep Maggie in reserve as a possible contact with the old world should she need one. She would go alone. She grew breathless with excitement. She paused to watch the antlers moving about in the alder thicket, down, up, down. Alone. Overhead, Canada geese were clanging south. This, the next phase of her life, would be her affair, a new one she'd play by ear, for sure.

On the rattly little plane to Dakhla, Marty read in the two-day-old *Times* an account of the children's peace run. He glanced down at wind-blurred dunes and felt lonesome and insignificant. He wondered what his brother was doing at that moment. He thought about Father Dmitri and tried to remember some lines from one of their sonnets. He envied William his deep marriage, even his paltry dramatic evanescent selfish hurtful engulfing affairs. He envisioned his brother's big padded shoulders square above the threshold, beneath the lintel of his farmhouse door; he saw Annette and their two children swimming like trout from room to room inside the house. Yes, he could imagine Annette as a teenager. High above Africa he partook of a silent mass that was filled with yearning and loss and sexual promise. Andrew was the gentle priest.

At the beginning of evening, before the moon has risen, the children's faces gleam. They push armfuls of air round them with as much ease as at the outset of the day; push air from ahead to behind with hands like fins or wings, step into the vacuum.

"We're running against racism!"

"Yes we are!"

"We're running against famine!"

"Yes we are!"

"We're running against war!"

"Yes we are!"

∞

In August Annette telephoned her mother because she was so upset she couldn't think straight; but she could not speak of this latest affair to her mother because her mother would have nothing to offer. And it had happened before, this phone call, this smooth agonizing conversation about the summer garden and next year's landscaping plans, this sinking feeling of being hurt and a failure and also perhaps too intelligent to let it happen again, but knowing that it had happened and would happen, that she'd wait through the helplessness, through all the lies and recomplicated lovemaking and guilty presents, until William returned, as he always did, like a nervous schoolboy screwing his uniform cap in his hands. Such a leaden feeling of being stuffed with words and words with no pictures, and the words themselves describing only themselves and evoking no image of anything. Such a black hatred of her garden and house where she worked with no satisfaction because she didn't know what else to do. Where she waited, blind even to the children, for William to return her life to her. So she left the phone and went crying into the good bottomland as she executed weeds and recounted to herself over and over the exact phrases of the semi-literate notes from this woman Faye she had just discovered and recognized instantly even before having opened the first envelope.

What she imagined of this woman Faye was a softly indented navel, taut skin of a narrow waist, a boy's bum. What she remembered of William was his fascination with early photographs of herself. Of Annette before William.

Now it would start, the obsession, though for him it had perhaps begun weeks ago. She didn't like to think of that. Without wanting to, she'd have to try to find the beginning. She'd have to recollect all their own meetings, conversations, intimacies of the early summer.

∞

"We are running against fascism!"

"Yes we are!"

"We are running against crime!"

"Yes we are!"

"We are running against corruption."

They're approaching borders, crossing borders, or cities, or installations. They belong to nobody; they've broken free. Soon they will fall asleep. In barns, in the middle of highways, beneath boat hulls, in olive groves, along river banks, inside arenas. Soon there will be heaps, small piles of the bodies of children, higgledy-piggledy, pell-mell, harum-scarum, in every slight depression on the planet's surface. All over the world they will fall asleep, soft limbs touching or overlapping, mouths open, exposed skin in a light sweat, not too hot, not too cold, muscles flicking to remember the run.

Maurice told William he'd spent his life in different towns parking next year's automobiles in banks, supermarkets, and shopping malls.

"Why?" said William. "What for?"

"Raffle cars, you know, prizes."

"Oh, I see." William looked at Maurice's worn jeans, his skimpy shirt. The man was in his early thirties, scruffy-clean, hard-looking, soft-spoken. Mart would find this guy attractive, he thought.

"Tricky jobs," said Maurice. "Some of them. Real tight squeezes. They want those autos in places make a guy scratch his head and wonder. Got to use your brain if you wanna park those autos someplace eye-catchy. They want a fucking magician with a bag of tricks. Maybe you build a ramp, take out doors or windows or handrails, maybe bang out a skylight, bring in a crane, rent a chopper."

The bus had been driving uphill for the past hour. Darkness fell long ago. Most of the handful of passengers still aboard were asleep. It was beginning to snow.

"I got no friends," said Maurice. "I have no girl and no home at this moment. What happens is I stay in a place too long I get so boring everybody gets sick to the stomach. When I have a girl she brings over her friends, see, to the place we are living, and for a while I have a place, I have a girl, and I have many different friends, all kinds. That is pretty nice. But then bingo I get boring, make the girl and everyone sick, so here I am. A guy needs to be alone. Like this. Alone and meeting other guys, also alone. This is deep and necessary shit. Charge your battery, man. Not that we could ever be buddies, you and me, but we have this little talk, this night, then next place we find other girls, new ones, yes?"

"God, I wish my life were as simple," said William.

"Yes, you are a big guy. Big professional married guy who makes too much money and gets lots of pussy. And on the side, too, yes? This is a short journey for you, I know. Not to make offence, but you are probably boring everyone, even if you don't know it, even if you're not so boring as me. Mother Mary, this time I got real boring."

"Huh," said William.

"Tell you what, man. Tell me about your wife. Your beautiful wife."

"Why should I?"

"We are running, man, but not like these children are running, but running from—"

"Oh, come on." William rubbed his neck and looked out at the black ditch, black trees. The bus's wipers were squeaking. The driver looked as though he were trying to break the wheel. "Is that your name? Maurice?"

"Maurice Montes. And you?"

"My name is William," said William. "My wife is Annette. And you're right, Maurice, she's beautiful. She doesn't think she is. I believe that is my problem. Her self-image."

"Yes. What she doesn't think is your problem. And she is big or small? She talk a lot?"

"She's naturally happy. Never worries. Never thinks about what might happen. She's guileless."

Maurice grunted.

"Ah well." William looked at Maurice's eyes. "My brother likes men—boys."

Maurice smirked. "The dirty scoundrel. Hey? The dirty scoundrel."

William shrugged. They both laughed. The bus pulled into a service station to which was attached a small café, gloomy inside.

The two men ordered coffee, then took turns in the restroom. Sitting at the counter, they watched the waitress—the only other person in the place—push a high stool into the shadows beyond the kitchen doorway and sit regarding them. They could see only her eyes.

William paid for the coffee.

He stood with Maurice by the parked bus. Snow was melting on Maurice's shirt and on the tattoo on his chest, but the lean man looked comfortable and was not shivering. The café lights went out behind them, and when the bus engine engaged and the door fizzed open, William realized that the night had been absolutely silent for the few seconds he'd stood watching Maurice in the snow.

# GULF

## 1.

Dear Mom,

Just a card to tell you I've left Alison for ten seconds of Marlon Brando. You said that I cried at sunsets when I was two years old. I'm doing it again. It's dawn, birds are singing, early trucks starting to roll, and I'm taping a movie. Been longer than I care to remember since I felt like crying at the beginning or end of anything. What else can I tell you? The desk top is cool formica. So long, Ma. I'm beat. I'll get some sleep. Today I will burn some miles—later today. Don't worry.

Your Charles

⌒

Dear Mom,                                          Trail, September 10

I landed a room with a view of the smelter and the people here seem friendly and funny. It's sad enough, though. At night everything smooths away flat and calm, and not even the mountains get in the way. Every moment is like one of the towns round here, boring as hell; the time between is only that: time spent driving between. I've had some pain in my legs so every evening I take a stroll in the parking lot, dragging my heels like Charlie Brown's friend Pig Pen but with a spiritual cloud. Mornings the people on TV don't even look like people. Blurred shapes crossing a room. The newscaster's cheerful eyes black with shadow peering deep into mine. How could I leave my children? How could I leave the clinic? Every night I hear the voices. Some I helped. Made them laugh. I helped parents keep alive their crazy hope. "Suffer the little children." Sweet Jesus.

Am I in real trouble? I watch a figure in an almost-empty landscape and I tremble. What approaches in the middle distance is not recognizable. There's a closeup of eyes.

Your son Charlie

☉

Dear Mom,                                    Rossland, October 20

How are you? The other day I taped more Brando (Fletcher Christian in *Mutiny on the Bounty*) plus a long sequence of *Star Trek* cut with *M\*A\*S\*H*, bits of a thing on spiders, and fragments from two other movies: *Sweat* and *Alien*. When I watch TV I feel all my insides coming out. When I see a pregnant woman I think my God the invasion has begun.

I left Alison because she dumps washer fuzz on the rhododendron by the back door and every week I have to wash the dried muck off the green leaves and when I speak she pretends not to hear and when I repeat myself she pretends not to understand what I've said and she deliberately stands behind me when I'm trying to pee and she pats me all the time for no reason. Just thought you'd care to know. Say hi to Dad. Tell him I'm joining a medical corps in Saudi Arabia.

Dr Chuck

Dear Mom,                    Revelstoke, November 21, 1991

I'm starting with a whole empty piece of paper so I can give you some idea of my present life. "Nuke the family," a trucker said this morning at breakfast. "Nuke the whole family of them," he said. He was alone and away from home, too, a big guy with tattoos and tired eyes. The waitresses were goosebumpy; beyond the big windows the river shone blue and sparkled. The trucker and I ate poached eggs, ham, hash browns, toast, and black coffee. Tonight in my room near the tracks freights wail and a hook-nosed televangelist shows news clips. Here's Brando's Kurtz, deep in Vietnam's jungle. Elizabeth Montgomery, young and pregnant, in *Bewitched*. Mohawk warriors in T-shirts cradling high-tech weapons. A black adolescent comedy actor with Bambi eyes. Euro-American kids running a beautiful suburban street in magic-hour light, going home for microwave dinner. U.S. marines edging round one another as if the world were a small crowded room. "Christ is not one of those heroic alloy brains riding the thin skin of our atmosphere," the evangelist says. "God is not a signal bounced once or twice off of a satellite."

Hear me, Jesus! I feel like yelling. I've got folds of skin where my legs join my body. Hear me, Lord! My thighs are so skinny, any fat looks alien. Hear me, Jesus! Hear me, Lord!

I went swimming yesterday afternoon. Stopped the car at a lake and broke ice in the shallows, went naked and had a vision. Can you hear me, sweet Jesus? I swam from shore toward the middle of the lake, buried my face in cold water, trying to remember all I knew about hypothermia, and saw the monster Pike, and saw the Pike seeing me. My little penis hanging like a juicy morsel in the heaven of Pike home, the fish flying up out of the depths, snub nose accurate as a missile. Swam a clean stroke to shore, pushing the water away, pushing it back toward that deep, that fearful place.

    Love Charles
    PS "The horror, the horror."

⌒

Dear Mom,                                                      Hope

Who are these happy little people on the talk show? They are
victims of a degenerative bone disease. What do they want,
these tiny victims of love, waving at the camera? If I could I'd
make love and violence unrecognizable, so we don't remember, so nothing in us remembers either condition. I want to be
taken in.

I was watching an interview with a reborn porn star, whose
sitting posture reminded me of Dad in his boat, when I lost
track of the star's story to dream of losing everyone, losing
Alison, you, Dad. On the road today I saw people for the last
time. On TV they are having babies and losing loved ones over
and over. Wind sweeps their hair over their shoulders. They
are bombing Baghdad. I've the feeling somebody is creeping
up behind me. "The desire to help is genuine." The porn star
sits erect, the ecstasy of redemption flooding his face as the
camera slowly zooms.

Though surgical strikes are intended, because of population
clusters there may be collateral damage. We sit out this dance,
while jets continue precision-bombing sorties, seek-and-destroy
missions, while B52s, FA16s, and stealth bombers deliver
payloads, and the tomahawk cruise hits time-urgent targets. I
don't know what is meant by anti-personnel or antidote. Men
on TV debate death estimates, psychological damage, friendly
casualties. In a busy Jerusalem hotel room the gasmasked CNN
cameraman shoots his face live in the vanity mirror. Man, oh
man. I have to go home. There's a woman on the screen as
smooth as a doll, as seamless and featureless, flat and impen-
etrable as a doll. I'm trying to see something new in the perfect tilt of her perfect chin. I'm cold turkey from my own life,
Mom. Isn't that the terrible addiction, one's life?

Your only begotten Charles

## 2.

"I love to use a camera on people," Charlie says to his guests. "I'm going to know all of you like the back of my hand." Flourishing his new Sony, he weaves in and out, catching every embarrassed reaction.

Alison, drink in hand, leans in the doorway; he swats her hip as he passes, records her astonished face.

"It's people I love," he says, shrugging. To the others: "I'll watch you all night on TV. Every night from now on I'll have you with me. Every evening when it gets dark I'll have everyone I know on TV, starting with you guys because you are my best friends."

Alison shakes her head. The others are tightly smiling.

"Ah!" He points the lens at the wives of two colleagues. "I'm sensitive to women, and I don't mean your faces or a compendium of your parts—I mean your ethos, the ethos of women."

"Shouldn't you be aiming your camera a different direction, then, sweetheart?" says one of the women. She gently but firmly nudges the lens aside. "Like away from us, toward what we might be looking at?"

Later, when the guests have left and he's made love three times to Alison and she's gone to sleep and he's edited his friends into one long happy sequence, he turns off the equipment, opens the curtains, leans back in his chair and locks his hands behind his head.

Now, he thinks, everything can begin.

The sky is dull grey with a slab of colour in the east that looks like a girl's face. Orion's belt pales as the light comes up. A grubby boiler suit hangs dripping from the line in next door's yard.

So far so good.

The neighbourhood will take on more colour.

Life is just pictures, bits of scenes piling up. He's found the secret and means to share it. But how? He pauses a second to savour. He's in his living room and it's dawn. Sparrows twitter outside, and early commuters are starting to roll. He's so awake it hurts. The oak desk is warm and golden. He'll phone his mother and wish her good morning, brush his teeth, eat some ice.

∞

Back home in Vancouver, returned to his job, Charles is alert. He's made a new start with his wife. With his eye on the Gulf crisis, he's investing heavily in futures. He wants to paint the house; he wants to take Alison back to where they met. Days seem brief and busy, though nights go slowly because he lies awake, tying up loose ends, trying to see his life as a gentle curve from the pink birth canal all the way to the end of his days. He phones his mother once in a while to update her on his recovery.

Charles and Alison take baths together, and as they towel each other dry they watch the suds collapse into water dark with their leavings. When it all runs out he says, "We're the real stuff, you and I. Hey, we'll be spending more than a few hours together. *I know what happens next!*"

He's interested in his body's appetites. He's finished with despair. He eats small amounts of good food and disdains sleep. No matter how many drinks Alison pours him, what pills she makes him take, how many times they make love, he won't sleep. With this much energy why close your eyes at night and why nap when the sun's up? These days, with trees bare, fog rolling off the ocean, short sad afternoons, he's feeling edgy in a way he's never felt before. "Muffled ecstasy," he says with a grin to the nurses at the clinic. "It's as if the world has meshed round me. I'm completely supported."

Alison wakes after a long drugged sleep and yawns into his sunny study.

"You don't look exhausted," she says. "How do you do it?"

"I'm in gear, darling. I cry at sunsets, didn't you know? I'm getting the hang of life. I'm doing one great job of work. I want you. I want to help my children. I want our own children. I want coffee."

"What's happened to you?"

"I'm right here." He flips off his monitor screen and beams at her. "And I don't need an excuse."

"Wouldn't you like to find out what I want?"

"Sure! Shoot!"

∞

Gasoline burns in engines all over the city. Leaves smoulder in drums by the side of the road. In the grate, kindling awaits a match. American troops amass on the borders of Iraq, watching the jets fly over. Low sun invades every room of the house.

Some patients into the day, Charlie is daydreaming of perfect skin grafts, his mind on continuous replay. He can't separate the children he doctors from news reports of the war. For a week there have been Iraqi scud attacks on Israel. He closes his skin graft dream and, deftly sewing up a rough cut in a child's leg, concentrates on the tissue healing beneath his fingers. Looking into the child's eyes, he's given a few dark scenes. Nothing clear, but the figures for an instant seem enormous, the event cataclysmic.

"You'll notice I didn't get far," he says to the nurse as he makes his way quickly down the corridor. He hands her the needle. "I've got an emergency. Industrial accident. You finish."

He leaves the building. In the minute it takes him to spot his vehicle, icy rain soaks his shoulders. Damp penetrates his coat, glues his shirt to his skin. The clammy fabric along his spine makes his head feel independent from his body. Once in the car he lets the large presences in the child's eyes manoeuvre him to a rooming house on the edge of an industrial park. The house, an old Victorian that at one time had been fixed up, is in need of paint and a new roof. Water pours from a leaf-clogged eavestrough onto rough cement front steps, and he has to leap through.

"This is a lovely room here," says the landlady. "With a view of the river," she adds. "And the factory's real pretty all lit up after dark."

He pays her two months' rent, and listens to her heavy steps as she descends the two storeys to her ground-floor suite.

Charlie stands in front of the window watching rain turn to sleet, sleet to snow, snow melt on the glistening blacktop. By five o'clock it's raining again, and he goes home.

Late that night, when he's alone in his study, it's revealed to him that he can achieve beautiful public healing. He has been given this pure, simple gift. The light of it burns steadily, burns in the largest possible sense of burn. He'll wear a saint's face, pass his fingers over the patient, and the healing will be subtle and quick. He need never repeat one patient's treatment on another. In his personal life as well as at the clinic, he'll do everything once only.

Already on fire, he goes into the room where Alison is sleeping, folds himself into bed, twitches up her nightgown and, putting his stiff penis inside her, oscillates fiercely, and comes before she has begun to respond.

"You're like a hummingbird," she whispers.

"I'm a tender trembler." He nibbles her ear.

Back at his desk he sees a movement outside by the buzzing street light. Beneath heavy rain falling from an expansive sky, a van has parked half on the sidewalk in front of his house. The drawing on the van's side is of a Viking guitarist surrounded by large-breasted women. Charlie aims the video camera through the window at the man pissing in loops into the overflowing gutter. On the tiny view-finder screen it seems a dance, some kind of rite. He stops the camera, puts it down, goes into the kitchen and tunes the counter-top TV to CNN. He slips the ice-cube tray from the freezer. Crunching ice, he watches the newscast for half a minute. A bedraggled cormorant stands on a black rock beside a black undulating ocean and tries to shake crude oil from its neck. The bird turns bright eyes toward Charlie.

The van is still parked when he gets back to his chair. A tow truck arrives, and a mechanic in white scrabbles under the hood while the man who was pissing claps his hands. He claps his hands in applause. Let's face it, Charles murmurs, what else can we do? Each clap is like one of those street lights; the space between is only that: space between. It's not holy, though, what the rocker is doing; it's mechanical—it keeps the hands warm.

∞

When Charles looks at the X-ray of the girl's lung in the radiology lab, it's a surveillance movie. The shadow is cloud cover between the moment the child is in perfect health and the moment she is sick. Charles emits a tiny groan. A silent explosion. His mind fills with debris. All sound waves decay eventually into heat waves. Charles knows he's metabolizing. He's not acting anymore. It doesn't matter whether or not he watches TV, reads the newspaper, or listens to the radio. He can no longer play a role, not in clinics or hospitals, not in emergency wards or consulting rooms. He's very close to some edge beyond which lies all the pain in the world. The OR is rhythm and organization. Although the amplitude of doctors is decaying, it continues to maintain that gorgeous order. All Charles is trying to do is fine-tune his treatment of himself, by breathing, walking.

∞

From his hideout suite he watches forklifts crawl the alleys of the factory below; he speeds them up, changes their patterns of interception, blurs them, fuses them together. He tells himself it's people at work; it's a nest of real men and women, not a gallery of machines—though machines and robots have his attention these days, with their jewelled mechanisms, brains full of switches. Smart machines are the antidote, they say. Patriots intercept scuds over Israel. He observes the workers in fading daylight put hard muscle against a metal and plastic device bigger than a person; the device eclipses four people standing beneath, reaching for the sky. The crane operator sits in a transparent room far above them, almost on a level with Charles.

After a while, the misted glass of the window gives Charles

the image of his own nose. His eyes black with shadow peer out each side. Because he's so close to his reflection and looking down, it's as if the lines of streets around the factory divide his face into zones. Dots of light cross his forehead. At a moment like this a technician on a jet would launch a missile. The late afternoon puts an end to the workers, reducing them to silhouettes. Charles touches the cross-linked zones of his face; soon they will open up like mission charts and show the way home to Alison. Will he be glad to see her?

The apartment also overlooks the river, which curls round the industrial complex. Charles, this night, reads from his own face and studies the river. He keeps trying to work out what happens between people, but he can't get it straight. These Iraqi attacks have no military significance. Indeed, what he has found from carefully watching the war and the factory is useless meaning. He feels the river winding by, no doubt polluted, yet passing nevertheless. Not unlike the children he sees every day; good places both to put his energy. Good places, deep and right.

∞

As rain, right as rain.

He sees seven children one morning, all of whom will die before they reach puberty. One working mother breaks down in his office, one father—what his mother would call a rough diamond—grasps Charles's hand with an iron claw and will not let go. They stand twisted together in the light from the window; the man's dry lips say, "Ah. Ah." When he's gone, Charles straightens slowly in the middle of the room till he feels he is the finished product. All gestures done. Childless.

Across the world we are burning children.

He is all surface. The interior of his house is being painted light green. He has a wife who loves him. He signals the nurse and attends the eighth child and finds that she will live, and this changes the colour of his eyes.

He'll wear the clinic like a second skin; he will love these children. They watch him take off their dressings in complete trust, and he listens to their hearts go to sleep beneath his hands. He soothes them, all of them, those he can heal and those he can't.

The parents are perforated; hope seeds itself in the fine silt that has filtered through, but it is their fear that blooms, that speaks and wants him to join their condemnation of whatever power directs their terrible worlds. Evanescent as a mote, his professional calm can now sustain every demand. Suffer the little children, sweet Jesus, sweet Charlie.

∽

Friday, Charlie buys a book on chaos dynamics, brings it home, settles in behind his desk, and reads the dust jacket. A ladder scrapes along the kitchen tiles. He calls the foreman of the painting crew into his study. The foreman takes off his baseball cap, and talks about the wrongfulness of euthanasia. The foreman wants to know if Charlie has ever helped anyone to die. He tells Charlie what should happen in the Middle East.

That afternoon, Charlie goes to the house of a patient who is near death. The boy's father insists that Charlie drink a beer with him in the living room. Through the window is a beautiful view of a mountainside transected by a logged slash. Charlie stands at the window and stares at heavy wires slung between dull pylons.

"Jerry is thirteen," says the father.

"I worked in Africa once," says Charlie.

"You know what my son wants? More than anything? He wants to fight in the Gulf War. He told me he wants to die with God, fighting for his country's rights."

Chaos dynamics, Charlie thinks. The way smoke coils in disturbed air. Wave patterns. Maybe the way beliefs of how the planet operates intersect.

"Jerry told us he'd trained his dog," says the father. "We've got a terrier. Jerry's spent hours training her. He told us she would dance when he sang, and last night he made us get him up, carry him in here and turn on all the lights. He sat in here with the dog and sang. The dog just went crazy. Round and round the carpet howling."

Charlie looks at everything inside the room.

"I want you to tell me how I should deal with his death," says the father.

Charlie takes a step toward the armchair where the man is slumped facing the window. His face is pale. The words were spoken in a voice so low and unaccented as to seem devoid of will. Charlie touches his shoulder. The frosted glass of beer is cinched between the man's thighs. His slightly curled fingers twitch open on the plush armrests. He expects no answer. His eyes are counting something, flicking left to right, left to right, his head nodding just perceptibly.

*Suntreader*, Charlie wants to say. *Men and Mountains* and *Angels* and *Suntreader*.

"I don't care," the man says. "I don't care."

"Nine pylons," says Charlie.

"What?" The man looks up, then gives an agonized smile. "Oh, yes. Nine."

A machine somewhere beneath the house starts to hum. The air in the room moves. Charlie smells the man's aftershave.

In the dining room a bed occupies one wall. The boy's body is a straight line, his cheek and the side of one foot snug to the cream plaster. The mother, at a folding card table beside the bed, is piecing together a jigsaw puzzle. The curled dog sleeps in the centre of the sky-blue quilt. The father exchanges a look with his wife, but stays in the doorway. Charlie sits on the edge of the bed. He's supposed to do something with his hands, to be brisk and cheerful, to move his hands in some sequence; but he can't remember: is he here to bless or to soothe? The boy's eyes are open.

"Any more scuds?"

"Not today," says Charlie.

"Has the ground war begun?"

"Not yet," says Charlie.

"Have they used gas?"

The jigsaw, three-quarters complete, is of an exotic bird, black and white, with blue webbed feet. Around the bird is a rock-strewn desert, or perhaps a shore.

Driving home, Charles superimposes the image of the boy and dog on the flat plane of the blue bed with the image of the power lines on the mountain. He imagines he hears the sound of the ladder scraping the kitchen floor integrated with that of the father's pallid bid for help. *Angels. Suntreader.* He wonders what kind of noise the blue-footed bird would make, and he begins to tremble.

∽

He's precisely, uniformly, reined in. Somewhere in him is a kind of joy, but he won't give it rein, because it might destroy him.

It's late the following afternoon, a Saturday, when he drives across Second Narrows Bridge, heading for his secret room. Some lives are more complex than others, he tells himself. This one's very complicated, almost chaotic. His mother and father have been bubbling in his gut since morning. When he was a kid, after they'd gone to bed, he'd stay up late switching channels. Watching the factory hour by hour opens a similar flower behind his eyes: beyond him a real, heavy-wristed longing suffuses the universe; the solar system grows still.

On the car radio, as he approaches the floodlit yards of the industrial district, he hears George Bush say, "Regrettably the noon deadline passed. . . . I have therefore directed. . . . The liberation of Kuwait has now entered a final phase."

He parks his car, climbs the stairs to his empty suite. He stands quietly, hands limp at his sides.

He begins, item by item, to empty his mind of thought.

Some X-rays remind him of other patients, children he's known, who have passed through his hands.

He's always been fascinated and calmed by a woman's figure in the middle distance.

By midnight the river glows in the dark, a phosphorescent snake. He has burned his gaze on this river; he feels the current's immanence; in his arteries he can feel the tug. And now his legs begin to throb. With each heartbeat they throb, till every muscle, every bone aches. He must force his legs to pump him round the room.

It hurts! Charley horse. Muscle spasm. Dear God.

But the pacing helps ease the pain. Oblivious of his surroundings, he clumps past the window, past the window, past the window.

It works. From his head, as he marches, is disgorged the *Star Trek* sequence cut with *M\*A\*S\*H*, the spider documentary, *Sweat*, and *Alien*. Soon he'll stop still, dead still; Marlon Brando will depart; the grass will stop growing.

He'll be nobody's son, will talk to no one, and all the people that see him will be happy because he's doing everything just right. They won't know all his goodness. They won't know the half of it.

And Alison. He'll say goodbye to Alison. Tears stream down his cheeks, glinting in the factory lights. He's running the edges of the room now, really pounding. At last he's come to love their life. No longer will she dump washer fuzz on the rhododendron; no longer will he clean the green leaves. It doesn't matter. His body feels like heated bronze; his thoughts are neon flashes seen from a great distance. Baghdad. She will never again, for any reason, touch him.

When the sun strikes his chest, he's trying to remember something.

Goodbye to Father. Forgiveness from Mother.

ⓒⅅ

This Wednesday evening, as he looks at his wife across the living room, he remembers the breakfast place where he ate exactly what the trucker was eating. He tries to tell Alison about the guy's tattoos and his tired eyes, about the poached eggs, ham, hash browns, toast and black coffee.

"I'm getting flabby, Alison," he says. "I've got folds of skin where my legs join my body."

He looks across the living room into his wife's eyes.

Alison stops what she's doing. She stares at him; but he feels only a tear run down his cheek.

"Oh Charles," she says.

"Alison," says Charles, "when will silence be an act of love?"

Alison goes into the kitchen, stands at the sink. "What are you talking about, Charlie?"

He nods. "My legs are killing me." Struggles to his feet.

In the kitchen doorway, he plays with the light switch. "If this is the house of love," he says mournfully, "then lack of desire is Charlie's sole *raison d'être.*"

"Are you feeling all right, Charles? Are you okay?" She sorts dirty dishes, throwing cutlery into the green wash bowl.

"Who are the heroes of the silent screen?"

"Why are you doing this?"

"I'd forgotten how many kinds of silence there are."

"Oh yes?"

"A lot of apples, a lot of doves and silk."

Alison turns her back, adjusts the hot and cold, her fingers in the water, testing.

"If I could make it all recognizable, Ali, make it so I can believe in something. I want to believe in something. I want to feel a little hope."

A bird hits the kitchen window and Charles and Alison jump in unison; together they stare at the black glass. She looks quickly at the tines of the fork she's holding. Charlie gazes from her face to the picture of his father's boat. He hopes the night bird was not killed. He imagines it swooping on, jarred, through the neighbourhood. Alison continues with the dishes. Breathless with pain, Charles wonders what she sees in him. Usually she leaves the dishes till morning. It's late and they both are tired. Whatever hit the window has left a version of itself, a faint haze, fan-shaped, on the glass. He can't rid himself of that percussive boom as the creature clipped the invisible barrier. He looks again at his father stuck under a magnet on the fridge. *Fishing with Dad.* When he peers out of the window, he sees the big dipper and automatically scans for the north star.

Nothing is strange, nothing new. Dimly, outside the window, despite the ache in his legs, Charles sees Alison, his mother and dad, nurses and children, Marlon Brando and the painter, the dying boy and his parents. There, pale in the nearly full moon, on the road outside his window. They are not mechanical, not real. Somewhere else, farther away, tires squeal. Through the hedge fronting their property, bright with new leaves, he sees the glow from the arc lights of the highway grocery. He feels wind sweep the tang of spring past his house and past all the houses on the block. He cranes his neck, still looking for the star. He can sense Alison creeping up behind him.

At the clinic, where he must help cure sick kids as well as he's able, the rooms are empty. The desire to save is genuine; but there is this need to pause, the need to gape, the need to hold everything, wide open.

In the window glass Charlie sees the reflected kitchen and Alison close behind him. He feels her breath on his neck. He clicks on the radio and they both hear, not the end of the war, but the announcement of a cease-fire.

# The Irish Photographer

When I asked him about the newspaper clipping photograph, Dad said it was taken at a Regent Street fashion show on a dull thirties Saturday afternoon in winter. He points out the chandeliers that hang from shop awnings, the pedestrians that crowd the pavements, the hero jumping the barricade right in front of the slow-walking ladies. Dad said Grandad told him the carpet was red and the lights flickered.

And everything blurs as the hero takes the most gorgeous model's arm, twirls her. And she doesn't miss a beat. And her white gown flares.

∞

When I was young I believed that Grandad went to Ireland to work as a photographer. That in the early thirties, after the Depression hit my dad's family in the north of England, that's how Grandad earned his bread. I imagined him among green hills, toting an old-fashioned camera like a great bat sleeping between his shoulders. When I discovered politics, I had him dodging bricks in a Belfast alley after curfew, the camera smaller,

133

the man larger. Recently I learned that though he'd worked in Ireland it was in his own trade, cabinet making. He did get employment as a photographer, but that was later, at the Ford Motor Company at Dagenham—London. His job was to patrol an iron walkway that hugged the inside factory walls far above the workers and take pictures of any man he saw loafing, pausing for a cigarette, gossiping.

∞

I can talk about my grandad in a way I can't begin to talk about my dad, who is too gentle, too alive. Of my dad I can only say he's about to retire. He has white flyaway hair and soft brown eyes. He's competent, reassuring, considerate—and simple, transparent, vulnerable, difficult.

∞

Grandad's boots rang on the grid floor of the balcony as he walked back and forth, but the sound was lost in the clamour of machinery. The men knew he was there, but no one looked up. Cars in various stages of completion filled his viewfinder. The man to whom he reported at the end of his shift was young and educated and clean shaven and a southerner and had a scar running down his left cheek. His name was Mr Simmons and he told my grandfather how much film he should be using, how many pictures he should be taking if he was doing his work properly. He spoke of men as his teams. Certain teams were slow, some chatted too much. Statistically so many men at each phase of production would be lazy. Some phases had bad records; painting seemed to encourage daydreaming. Fumes and poor ventilation were a problem. On his wall Mr Simmons had a map of the factory with different colours to represent the range of efficiency. He had a graph comparing production figures here with those of a factory in America. He had diagrams of different methods of assembly. A list of his teams, of the men in each team. All this he showed my grandfather in the relative quiet of his tiny office. On his desk lay the folder of photographs. If a man on opening his pay packet found his picture (black and white, grainy, aerial view) he'd know he'd but one more chance. No one but Mr Simmons talked to my grandfather, and Mr Simmons talked in an arrogant fashion, soliciting no response. The men on the floor knew nothing of my grandfather's life. They shunned him because they couldn't imagine anyone that desperate.

He lived in a boarding house in the dock area south of Barking and rarely spent any time in London. He sent much of his pay home every week. He wrote brief letters to his two teenage daughters, to his wife, and to my father who was not yet ten, who was the spoiled baby of the family. Sundays he walked by the warehouses along the river. When he spoke in shops his accent labelled him a foreigner, from up north, a bit thick. Many men were drifting then, and he drank his Saturday pint with other exiles in pubs in Ilford and Upminster. They spoke in whispers of the football teams each supported, their longing for home. He joked with girls in the pubs, looked in envy at childless men whose wives were with them, and missed his children. He belonged to his family and to Sale near Manchester and to Manchester United, not City. One day he quit the job, quit London, came home saying he couldn't take it any more, could no longer stomach it—but neither could he afford to settle. He transferred his belongings to a trunk and, while Grandma mended his clothes, he kissed his daughters and shook his son's hand. He went to America. In Minneapolis he bought a gold watch, a clear-faced watch that eventually would stick at twenty-five past twelve. He stayed only a matter of months before sailing home. He was a quiet and tight-lipped man. He did not travel abroad again. Never in his life did he go farther than America, but at the Ford Motor Works he must have dreamed all the time of that country. In Dagenham, each time his finger made the shutter open, he went to America. Just for that second the noise faded, the men froze: they guilty of woolgathering, he of noting their dreams. And all the while cars continued to take shape, and smoke to drift across remote skylights, till the factory was infinite and bottomless, all shadows, crawling shadows; and it was ominous, passing strange, that in the sparks and fumes and glare he couldn't make out the men.

Away from his family, a job he loathed. His belly hurting by day, and nights to sleep with a headache.

For news of America, he'd pay a visit to the library on his day off. Not a socialist or a deep thinker, but a worker, middle lower middle class, down on his luck.

I remember a surly man sitting in the parlour corner of the house where my father grew up. An old man in a waistcoat on a straight-backed chair. His arms folded. Waiting for his Sunday tea. He said nothing, while Grandma, paralyzed down one side, carried washed greens from the kitchen sink to the chopping board, her feet shuffling on the uneven flagstones. He gave me a box of junk to sort through—I would find treasure. He watched me on the rug pull out this and that. He had a word for what I did—rummage or root. I remember him dying, but not his death.

∞

Later. Grandma sick in bed in the room next to the parlour, a deep room with velvet upholstery, heavy curtains across the front windows and also across the middle of the room. My sister and father and mother present but invisible. The electric fire on, all three bars, a smell of singed dust. Buried in cushions, the face of my grandma white above the tall bed. Her bad hand crooked, pushed under the eiderdown.

Her house and ours were put up for sale. The family would steam west from Southampton. But at the last minute Grandma refused to go to Canada. Perhaps she hoped we'd return in a few months as in the thirties Grandad had from London and then from the New World. But we settled in Vancouver, she in her new old folks' home. A couple of years after we emigrated we received a photograph of her: she's tall and thin, her hair as white as Dad's is today. Night and Christmas and a flash have caught her smiling under the holly, dancing in the rest-home dining room with a small old brown man, her cane nowhere to be seen.

☙

Down south Grandad's belly hurt. Every night he tried to walk off a headache before going to sleep. Head low, chin almost resting on his chest, he tramped and tramped.

One day toward the end of summer—a hot September evening, not a breath of air—he found his path blocked by children playing British Bulldog along the pavement. Working class children. Boys on boys' backs yelling like lunatics, all in shabby serge school uniforms. The mounted clawed at one another while their steeds lunged and toppled. Their voices hurt his head. He escaped into a sweet shop and bought ten Woodbines; he stole a chocolate bar and a packet of envelopes. When he came out he was crying.

☙

Grandad changed his clothes weekly till they wore out. He buttoned a shirt, fastened his braces, remembering where everything came from: trousers from the Sally Ann, socks and underwear from home, jacket and vests from his widow landlady. Today pyjamas from the landlady. She left things in his room while he was at work. He thanked her silently. Blessed his wife for warm socks. Blessed the poor and the Salvation Army and the dead who had no more use for their trousers. He shook water from his brush and replaced it on the white doily on the chest of drawers, pressed the horn comb diagonally into its bristles.

☙

Where exactly he tramped, he couldn't say. He didn't connect his tramps with the rest of his life. His route to work was a going somewhere along certain streets, while his tramps went nowhere along any street. Tramping, he never recognized a landmark, because he wouldn't lift his head. It was pavements he saw and what was on them, shoes, his own shoes. The shoes he polished every night that always seemed dusty. He wouldn't have much more in his head. Wouldn't think of anything but the generations of his shoes and where and when he'd acquired them. When he reached the end of a street he crossed to the other side, turned round and walked back to the beginning and crossed and walked the route again. On one long street his turning point was the brick design under the sweet shop window. On another it was the building site where somebody had painted words in blue enamel low on the boards. He'd half-close his eyes and smell London earth, London clay, right there.

But the kids. The kids in uniform not letting him through.

Into the shop he'd gone. An old lady, a Londoner, stood four-square behind the counter. A baby sat on top, taking bits of plum from a girl the age of his eldest. He snatched the chocolate bar and envelopes off a shelf when the old lady reached for the fags. The girl saw him, but said not a word. She had on a blue pinafore. Her mouth was red with plum. Her eyes looked right into his. He felt his fingers curl into fists. He paid for the Woodbines.

"Ta."

The girl said, "Bye, mister."

The baby said, "Bye, mister."

Outside, the city blurred. His pockets were burning. And he couldn't move left or right, till he remembered which daughter had sewn the initials on his handkerchief.

∞

The dance takes in the whole street, maybe the whole of London, with men waltzing tailors' dummies to an orchestra playing Strauss. White-collar workers lean from office windows over the street. "A bevy of beauties at a fashion show," the cutline reads. The hero, dressed in top and tails, plunges to the heart of the affair, right into the fashion show lights, right across the red-carpeted runway. He takes the model in his arms, twirls her through the dancers. And she daintily holds the hem of her white gown above the dirty pavement and no, she doesn't miss a beat.

One Friday dusk when Grandad leaves work the cold clasps him and squeezes till he's chilled through. Winter's smoke, damp and acrid, stings his nostrils. The stretch of river visible beyond the buildings is thick with yellow bubbles that shine through the dark. At the back of the factory he stumbles over a cat asleep in the slag between the scrap containers and the warm brick wall. A man slinks from the shadows, steps in front of him, tries to take his arm. In the harsh light from the doorway the man's face looks like a clown's: sweat and dirt have left a pattern of vertical lines on his forehead, his cheeks. He's shivering and looks desperate.

"Want a treat?" He pulls from his pocket a flat blue box. "Real bargain."

"No. Go along."

"Charge you hardly nothing, sir," he says. "Let's say three-pence to you—half price. Look! Lovely treats. The whitest skin! Here, put your fingers right in the little box. You like the ladies, sir?"

My grandad takes a picture from the box.

The man winks. "By yourself, cock, ain't you? By yourself and far from home." He nods toward the invisible city out past the smear of water. "There!" he says. "Cosy up in Toff Town. When I was a nipper we near froze waiting for the changing of the guard at Buckingham Palace. History in front of your eyes. Tell you what, mate. I don't like to tap a family man, and you got it written all over. Let's say three for a tanner. I'm old and poorly but I envy you. If I had my time again I'd have children and grandchildren, I would, and before this country's done see them lie down with the lions and the lambs. Mark my words, mate, there'll be deer drinking at the Thames again before England's finished!" He staggers a few feet, about-faces, then he's gone.

"For she is the gal," his voice comes singing back, "with the two-dollar smile, and the five-dollar eyes!"

My grandad stops still in the dark, listening. Minneapolis in his hand: a boy in striped pyjamas half lying on a girl with an icy grin whose camisole straps have slipped, whose black hair gleams.

∞

And the dancing, as though it's not a cold grey London day, is thunderous, full of colour and light.

∞

Winter Saturday afternoon in the city, Grandad, postcard in his pocket, goes out—he was in a hunting dream last night— goes out to investigate job opportunities in America. And it's not British Bulldog blocks him this time, but some kind of beautiful pantomime, the children grown up. He remembers the sweet shop, the stale sweet chocolate bar, the envelopes all gone but one, all but one sent north, and the one left containing the postcard of Minneapolis. He reaches for his breast pocket beneath his scarf, his new scarf from home. He can't believe so much gaiety, such a red carpet. He's on a stage, in a parade, surrounded by tired men with briefcases, shopper women, newspaper boys, lovely statues. Right now he's hunting in a dream, can't help it. It's an omen. It's nineteen-thirty-one coming. He's a lover in striped pyjamas, and a family man. God blesses the meek and the mild and the gentle and virtuous. These dancers are his beaters. His mind is troating a buck, a buck on the banks of the Thames, all the way to the forests of America. He'll tell Mr Simmons to stuff his job. Niagara Falls in his sights! He'll cross the Atlantic, and his family will follow. The sky tinted blue.

He's so chuffed he walks straight to the nearest public house and downs a whiskey.

Except for a young couple finishing their drinks, putting on coats, the place is empty of customers. A woman is writing in a ledger behind a half-partition at the back. The traffic outside is muted here. He orders again. He wants to talk to someone, but the publican will only polish glasses and pour his drinks. Grandad turns to watch the woman's hands on the accounting paper—her right smoothing the page ahead of the left as she jumps columns. He can't see her face, but she has a small head, pretty brown hair. He won't attract her attention by speaking or approaching. Her fingers smooth along, drop a line, begin again. She's too immersed in her figures to hear his feet shuffling under the bar, his quiet coughs. He pulls hard on his cigarette, gulps his drink, cracks it on the counter. In the end he goes to her. Hands in pockets, he works his way to the partition, steps in front of the desk. She glances at him, draws a quick breath, twitching the way a sleeping person steps from a cliff.

"I'm sorry to frighten you," he says.

"You startled me," she says.

"Working?" he says.

"Aren't we clever."

"Hard luck working on a Saturday."

She shrugs, carrying on with the numbers. He makes as if to go, then doesn't.

"Me, I get Saturday afternoons off. Real shindig down Regent Street, dancing and all. Should've seen it. I'm going to the library. I want to find out about jobs in America. I'm thinking of going there, to America."

"Oh, yes?" she says.

"I'm with the motor works now," he says. "Dagenham. It's fine, but . . . No work north, you see. I've a wife, two girls and a boy up Manchester."

"Good for you, then."

"Aye. A bloke must look after his own. No work north, d'you see. I've a picture of the family . . . "

"Look, I really am busy," she says.

"You wouldn't maybe like to have a cuppa with me after you get finished here, would you? Just for a chat, I mean. I don't mean, I mean to say—"

"Sorry," she says. "No, I couldn't do that. Sorry."

Grandad takes a hesitant step away.

"Go on now, love," she says. "Best of luck at the library! And good luck in America!"

Grandad retreats to the counter where an excited customer, a tall fair-haired pale young man, is ranting at the dour publican. Grandad decides he'll have one more, even if it means he'll be broke and will have to walk home.

The publican stares at the young man, listening, frowning. He pours Grandad's drink and takes the coin without looking at him. The newcomer stamps his feet as he speaks. He's wearing a thin overcoat and still trembles with cold, and, to judge from his features, he's the publican's son. His voice is clipped, and even though he struggles with his words, it's clear he's had education, and it's plain and obvious he feels he knows better than his old man.

∞

And now I see all the fathers walking backward in heavy traffic, facing the receding world, that crazy splendid world they've just made up, just laid out, and there they are, backing up, backing away, backing into dangers they can't see. They look so confident. They look so polite.

∞

"Of course," the pale young man at the pub continues, "it's you who are to blame, you don't need me to tell you you should go and see her, but oh no not bloody likely, that's too tough. How many times have you told yourself it's her fault not yours, if she'd been different, been this way instead of that, you wouldn't have had to give her the boot—"

142

The publican leans forward and gazes through the window at the road. He nods dreamily. "Like as not," he says, "like as not."

"Drink up, brother," the pale man says to my grandfather. "You look starved. Drink up! Well, here's luck to us. Here's to the gentle life. Nice it is when things are hunky-dory."

"Cheers," says Grandad.

"Bottoms up," says the pale man, turning back to his father. "Not working though, is it? Blaming her. Hasn't worked for bloody ages. I am right, aren't I? I am right? It's too late, is what I know. You've always been a bloody bull in a shop, and now you've broken everything and you wonder why it's all a mess, why the spoon's empty and you're in this sad hell, this place here. For God's sake. Tell me one thing, tell me you were happy once. You can remember you were happy once, can't you?"

"Yes," says the publican. "Yes, I was. We both were happy."

"Go and see her, Dad," says the pale man. "She looks terrible. Please go and see her."

"You don't know a thing," says the publican. "It started a long long time ago. Best not to think on it." He turns to my grandfather. "Another?"

"Ta. No."

"On the house," says the publican.

"Aye?" says Grandad. "Thanks very much."

"She makes your black pudding, bacon dumpling," says the pale man, "and she gives you a son, and you think you are all right, God's in his heaven, you can treat her—"

"Not here, lad," says the publican. "Not now."

"Your bloody pub, you know what it is? I'll tell you. I'll tell you. One lonely bastard of a paying customer. Open your eyes, Dad! Your own wife, you can't even go and look at her, can you?"

The publican is shaking his head.

"You make me ill. Look at you. Do I have to tell you what my mother looks like? Shall I? Shall I tell this poor bastard here, shall I tell your only bloody customer—"

"Go on home, there's a good boy. Go on, now. I won't say it twice."

The pale man turns and strides into the street. My grandfather and the publican remain, still a minute, elbows on the wood. With a steady hand, the publican pours himself and Grandad a drink. Grandad feels dizzy. He wants to jump a train, return to his wife and children, but he can't. He wants the money for America now, but there's barely enough just to live and send north. The woman behind the partition touches her pen to her lips and watches them.

"The thing of it is," the publican says, "he's quite right. Heaven knows. I won't mention who paid for his schooling and I don't regret it. That's well and good. That's fine. Fine. The thing of it is I do keep remembering his mother, seeing her, you understand, except it's always this particular occasion, oh ages ago, just one time in a million, and nothing special either. She's giving me a bit of a kiss and cuddle in the kitchen, nothing indecent, just a bit of a kiss and a cuddle. He's a baby in his crib asleep and it's a winter evening, freezing outside, and I'm trying to do something, fix something that's spread over the table, and she's got herself between me and it, she's in the way, but I don't really mind. I don't really mind. So there we are, we're stopped like that in the middle of the kitchen, her hanging on and me waiting it out patient-like. And I start flapping my arms, like a bird, you see, like a daft bird. I'm flapping and she's cuddling and laughing, and I say, 'Aggie,' I say, joking-like, 'Aggie, what a bird we'd make, what a bird.'"

# Pickled Eggs

I used to think I had intelligent conversations. I thought I had thoughts that made sense and went deep and when I sent them out as words they snagged other people. Even now from time to time I think I have something to say, maybe not original or penetrating, but smartish, not too dumb. Just an hour ago, in fact, I was talking on the phone to Jerome and got the old feeling. There I was, convinced we were on the verge of some valuable dialogue. He stuttered a bit; I gave a good response. Of course it was first thing in the morning, and maybe coffee was acting on our innards, but just for a second things were humming. Friends in school, Jerome and I. Graduated high school together. Then for the next couple of summers we played guitar and sax and laughed a lot and talked about girls and tried to meet them—not too hard though, because at that time we were enough for each other. We were, I believe, in love, if that's not too strong a word. How I miss him! And being twenty, how I miss that! Our talk today reminded me of the closeness we once enjoyed. Who knows, maybe with a little more effort we could've reached that certain level of communion. We live a bus ride apart, and when we meet it's usually by accident and it is awkward. On the phone we exchange advice on practical household matters, plumbing, drainage, forced hot air versus radiant heat, that kind of thing. He tells me about his kids and his studio work. The best we can do is have a snort and a chuckle or two. We never talk of the past or relive our youth, thank God. One day I should call him up and tell him how I used to feel about him. Perhaps we could arrange to spend a whole weekend together, the way we once did. I don't play sax anymore, but we could listen to Jerome's music. We could go for a walk. Cook a mess of spaghetti and eat it with buttered toast. I'd like to have intelligent conversations with Jerome again. I'm going to. All that we had can't just be gone. I'm sure we both used to think we had something really important to say. I knew I was confident I had a lot to offer. It's sad now to find—and not only with Jerome—that it takes all my concentration just to listen. When it's time to put in my two cents I'm not ready. I go fishy-mouthed. When I do finally dig up a word it sounds stern and cynical. My wife says that a good listener's a fine thing to be, a rare item. The thing is, I seem to have lost my confidence. I've been listening to the talk show hosts, comparing stupidities, trying to boost my self-image, but I'm still not sure I've much to say. It could be true, couldn't it? That I've said all I'm going to? But boy oh boy sometimes I want to really stretch and speak some golden words to touch a few people out there. Could be just nostalgia brought on by Jerome's stutter. Maybe it's just one day, then the next. Then again, maybe after a whole lot more listening, I'll have a load to get off my chest and won't feel tongue-tied. Listening, right now, maybe it's an experiment.

What?

My wife calling me to breakfast. It irritates her when I get dreamy—childless as a motherless child, she puts it, as if that makes any sense.

Soft-boiled eggs, free range. Holy yellow!

We look outside and say, Green grow the grasses, oh!

The rest of the meal is taken in silence, except when I try: Everything looks different in spring, which she answers with one of her terrific *mms*!

When I used to be in love I made sense. With Jerome, then a few girls, then my wife. Everything made sense. When Jerome and I spent days together and were half asleep after jamming all night, we said and thought the deepest things. Now I talk to the loans manager, the keypunch supervisor, and the guy who drives the pound truck. When I'm building the fence, I have a few words with the miserable neighbour. I go blank and sweaty every time.

Don't get me wrong. I still love my wife, and I have a warm spot for the pound guy, the way he handles those mutts. And I'm proud of my fence. Been building it for eight years now, section by section, using cement footings, pressure-treated four-by-fours and two-by-fours, cedar one-by-six rails, little cedar caps on the posts. That fence encloses the front yard, and soon will enclose the back. No wind will knock it down. Against it I plant sweet peas and annual morning glory every spring and will continue to do so even if my wife thinks it looks a mess after the flowers. She prefers lawn, cut real short, fence to fence, not a weed in sight, green in August. Every place else is lawn.

Jerome is not in favour of six-foot fences, no sir, and his wife hates lawns. This was the content of our recent conversation. I phoned him before breakfast to ask his opinion on the new *Four Seasons* where the violinist improvises, and he said he hadn't heard it. Then he asked what I was up to, and that's how we got to fences and grass. Unneighbourly, he thinks, six-foot fences. Darn right. But I told him I'm going to finish it anyway. He said his wife has dug up every scrap of turf at his place, and she and their kids are planting a huge vegetable garden. And she's organized the whole block, convinced all the neighbours to take down their fences and plant one massive garden. To change the subject I said, So how are the kids? And it happens. The tremble-zone. Over the phone, just for a moment, as he's telling me about his son and daughter and starting to stutter and I'm saying take it easy, we are so close. But then one of us, I can't remember who, starts to talk about fences again. I won't ever ask his help, physical or economic, for anything. I won't be beholden to Jerome, ex-

147

cept to listen to his music when he records it and offer my criticisms, which he can take or leave. There has been in the past, to be truthful, some competition between us, but I don't resent his small musical successes, as he seems to think I do. Just because we've gone different directions. He should leave my fence out of it. If he wants to talk to his next-door neighbour he can lean over his carrot patch and do so—I have nothing in common with mine. All that crumby guy does is water his drive and chain smoke.

My wife is flustered when I frown at the pickled eggs in my lunch box. She knows immediately why I'm frowning. We've arranged our menus to avoid excessive cholesterol, and eggs twice in one day is strictly forbidden.

Oh, shit, she says. Let me fix you something else. What was I thinking?

I say, We do seem a bit distracted today. But don't go to any trouble. I love pickled eggs. It won't hurt this once.

Here we are staring at two greyish eggs in a ziploc. She's put little twists of salt and pepper in the box beside them. The clock on the wall is ticking. It's really too late for her to make a substitute for the eggs. I'd defend my wife's lawn to the last green blade. I imagine talking her in my arms and kissing her, but last night my bicycle tire was flat and I must go and pump it up. I have barely enough time before riding to work.

Goodbye, I say, and she says, Goodbye, be careful in the traffic. Watch for parked-car doors.

What a trivial thing to say. She means it, though, and I appreciate the concern.

I like the dark, earth-smelling basement. My tools, shiny on their hooks. What I said about Jerome's criticisms, I don't know, I guess if I can criticize his music then he can criticize my fence. Probably his comments are as sincere and free from any past envy or resentment as mine are. And why should I argue for lawns when I'd give anything to dig ours up and plant wall-to-wall sunflowers?

Cycling to work isn't the big exercise deal I make it out to be. Less than a mile to the office, and level all the way. I should do long rides. Strap a tent on the back and take off for a long weekend.

Air smells so good in spring.

All the birds singing.

I used to think I was a good-looking person. I still think I look okay, I guess. But usually I think I will look better tomorrow. Get out in the sun, lose a few pounds, buy a new pair of jeans, some stylish T-shirts. Maybe start wearing a scarf knotted round my neck like I used to when I was twenty. Get my hair cut so it looks interesting. Put on beach-scene underwear.

What do I have in my life that Jerome would be envious of anyway?

Carefree existence, yes certainly. Free time, sure. My loving relationship with my wife. I've a suspicion his is not so great—he spends so many days away from home.

There's my legs pumping slow. Bet I'm in better shape than him. There's my strong hands gripping the handles. Barked my knuckles pruning the tree. Jerome won't get personally involved in such work in his yard. Says he might injure his fingers and lose his livelihood. I've got my hawk eyes on all those parked cars. We never used to be so cautious, none of us. Cautious isn't what I mean, I'm pretty sure.

Not much of what we think is what we should say, seems to me. Not much of what we say to one another is what we mean, either. We used to make sense, plain English, next thing we know we're all mixed up and can't express ourselves. Who knows why?

At least we're not at each others' throats.

On Monday after work I fixed a sand pit for the kids down the block at the bottom of the empty lot, and now as I wheel past I can see that little pink lakes have wept up where I dug, and the kids are standing round with their hands in their pockets. I don't know why I'm feeling so churned up this morning. I quit smoking years ago, but I'm thinking that a smoke and a coffee when I get to the office will set me straight, though what I want is someone to stop me dead, stop me in my tracks, and make an important announcement.

On the phone I've never had an intelligent conversation in my life, come to think of it, never heard and never passed on a word of wisdom, and I don't expect it'll ever happen. What happens is the phone rings, I pick up, open my mouth, and out pop all the habit phrases, and it's these, these little masks, that seem worse than anything; they are the end of the world, and saying them makes me feel glum, and as to how they strike the person on the other side, well.

# Crèche

In the middle distance, snow sheep. A black horse on a hill a long way away. But the children want the colours of autumn; each shuffles from the window to sit before a piece of paper and draw Rainbow Jesus with Mary and Joseph. Then, urged by Ellie Jones to fill the world with gentle animals, they populate the emptiness with the strangest shapes, knowing that at home everyone will recognize instantly what is given a name.

"In the Canary Islands it is warm, even in winter." Ellie Jones sighs. "South of the equator right now wild giraffes and kangaroos are enjoying summer."

Outside the window the snow goes on forever without a track. Every road to every city has disappeared, every telegraph pole, fence, dustbin, car. Up above Wales only stars shine in the dark sky. The children slip from their desks, gather at the side of the room, press their cheeks together, rub mitts across the steamy glass, and stare out. Nothing but white and black until their gaze crosses the valley to the twinkling lights.

Ellie Jones looks over their heads at the cluster of houses. Hers is the one with alternating blue and green fairy lights picking out the rail of the widow's walk. She put the Christmas

151

pudding to simmer this morning; it will greet her when she opens the door. She will listen to carols as she makes eggnog, and Kermit will come in yelling, Snow again tonight. She'll restrict him to his office while she sews presents. Next Christmas she will make a baby's small shirt or dress.

The night began at five in the afternoon; now it is six and still the children have not made a move to go home. Over and over they return smiling to their desks, move snail crayons across paper, then up again to confirm winter outside. Ellie Jones, like a weather doll, glides between her table and the window.

She remembers the Christmas her mother died—her first real Christmas; she'd have been about the age of these children. She and her sister went by train from Great Falls to Los Angeles to stay with their grandparents; their Jehovah's Witness father stayed home to mourn.

The oil furnace roars, while curved blackness settles like a vast leaf over the little schoolhouse. Ellie tells of the rogues and pirates who rage beyond the cold that surrounds the village. "They are wicked," she says, "and they sprout white swords and cut at one another in frustration at not being allowed inside a world they have almost forgotten existed."

The thoughtful children ignore her, draw instead what has yet to happen. Mam and Dad, siblings, roses. Seaside in summer. The loves they will have, the surprise visitor who smells of smoke, a table with every wonderful food imaginable.

In a wood in the next valley Kermit Jones and all the fathers harvest Christmas trees. They dig away the snow, gently ease roots free, transplant the young pines into a sleigh filled with earth. No one comments on how dark it has become. They work in silence, stopping only to throw a handful of oats into the horses' nosebags. Dressed in heavy black clothes, lips chapped and fingers aching, they sneak quick glances at one another. Soon they will go home, trudging beside their miniature forest on skis. One by one they rise up, stretch both arms high and, as if to assist circulation, clap hands.

At the window, this time looking only at the sky, the children listen. Ellie Jones is wondering about breast feeding, toxic waste; a disposal plant is to be constructed come spring, the largest in the country.

Mothers in the village on the hill run from room to room, afraid suddenly of avalanche. Every room is lit, still, waiting.

"Across the Atlantic," says Ellie Jones, "lives my sister. Her name is Miss Shirl Mortimer. I will telephone her tomorrow morning, Christmas morning."

Shirl works in a supermarket and believes in afterlife. She has always lived in Great Falls, Montana, and she has always had visions of animal ghosts. As she operates the cash machine she stares into space and sees things. The groceries that pass through her fingers make her see things, and she feels wistful and afraid.

She sees ghost cows lowing in iron stalls. Crying for their red decorations, for the ribbons they won at the county fair. Pining for their own little lives in the warm fields, a calf to nuzzle, shade for noon.

She sees turkeys rise up like smoke from their trussed white frozen forms, from the white freezer casks, noble, mean and beautiful even in death.

Yes, and in Great Falls, according to Shirl, the chickens are truly sad. She has heard they try to hide eggs, eggs under their downiest feathers, though the eggs are already gone, already in cartons on the supermarket shelf. "Next to lobsters, these battery chickens here," Shirl says, "must be the foolest most lonesome creatures in creation."

But the lobsters are crowded together in bright shallow empty tanks with their claws taped shut. Nothing to eat, nowhere to go, waiting to be chosen. And to think, two days past they were hunting in dark lovely sea! At times the supermarket feels as if it's raining light. Everyone moves slow and lazy. It looks like the morning before a country wedding. The lobsters are groomsmen waiting for the ceremony to begin.

It is so cold this time of year in Great Falls that outside in the parking lot motors are left running to keep warm.

"Once upon a time," says Ellie Jones, "there was a Christmas. And a child was born who could sleep so well that it won medals."

It had a way with dreams, a feather touch, and was beautiful to look at. The father loved the child and the mother loved the child; but the mother loved the child best, for the father first loved the world. To start, the child was content to sleep. Nothing made it happier than to dream while dust dusted down from high places. And the mother was happy too, though she sneezed a lot.

When the child woke it found nearly everything too rough for its delicate flesh. Its skin so soft that even the flies that the mother brushed away with ease left grooves. It could play only with old used-up bits of the world without getting cuts and bruises.

By and by the child began to long for the high places the father had access to. As it tickled fluff and old leaves out of the open door, the child dreamed of the shelves and filing cabinets of the remote corners of Heaven.

The child realized it was special.

A sensitive child, very clever.

Why shouldn't it explore the ledgers of its father's house?

And once that thought came, the child knew it would not be satisfied until it had joined the father.

It wanted to go and stay in the high places.

The mother heard and was impressed, then sad, then angry.

Dust mice scampered the floors, spiders made enormous webs across doorways, and every day the mother cleaned and polished in a frenzy, while the child sat on the carpet and plotted an escape.

The child devised a plan.

To win its father's love.

Ellie Jones shuts her eyes. She met Kermit Jones in a Great Falls bus shelter. It was late at night, and the schedule had been obliterated by vandals. No bus came, neither hers nor his, and they sat side by side, heads lowered, and talked for hours. By the time they decided to walk home, the shelter seemed a warm friendly place. A bench on dirty pavement in a glass enclosure. But room enough and chance for a conversation to range wide. He was an accountant sightseeing the Rockies, she a brand new teacher. Everything now, including her name, stemmed from that bus stop. Nothing has happened since—nothing beyond the plans made there.

"There was a new kind of feeling in the world," whispers Ellie Jones.

A love feeling.

But sad, because outside where the mother couldn't protect the child were mountains of dust, ferocious dust, by-product of the father's dangerous love, a powder that attacked the insides of people and made souls blind.

"On the other hand," as Cat Palmer would say, "maybe not."

Cat Palmer is the name Ellie Jones does not want to think about. He lives in Great Falls, and he is Shirl Mortimer's forever and always scoundrel darling, but he was Ellie's first time sweetheart. He was and is a reprobate in America. There are only two living people across the Atlantic, and Ellie wants to forget this one.

Cat.

Cat Palmer has one hundred dollars earmarked for Shirl Mortimer's Christmas present, and just now he almost spent it on a hooker, a long-legged child in long blonde hair, all because Shirl hasn't been good to him in over two weeks. A temptation. Ah, but he loves Shirl, and this proves it. How does it go, the old Christmas story? The guy pawns his watch to buy his woman a comb, and she sells her hair to buy him a watch chain? Would that mean Shirl is working the street for money to buy him a gift? Or perhaps another story applies here. Cat is always on the edge of some story. Maybe the blonde is turning tricks so she can buy someone she loves something nice. The guy is always passionate and the woman doesn't feel like it, or the woman comes on strong and the guy is blue. A big gust of wind sweeps the Christmas Eve shoppers along the sidewalk. Cat Palmer scratches his head and glances sideways before pushing open the door to the boutique. Still there, the blonde.

He rubs his eyes and looks at all the mirrors and all the girls and all the mannequins in flimsy clothes, and he doesn't have the remotest idea what to buy his girl.

Suddenly through the window he sees Jeremy Potts, descendant of the famous Indian guide and tracker, and he rushes out into the cold, grinning with relief.

Jeremy Potts, who has been hungry for days, has been watching TV in a bar downtown, and now he wants to know from Cat why he can't live in a house, in a village, have a wife and children, a few animals to tend.

And Cat says, What of it? So what? Don't we all want that but not really?

Before the snow fell snowberries marked Jeremy's night path through the park trees. Now after drinking he guesses his route, leading Cat the way his forbear led the Royal Canadian Mounted Police, cursing when last summer's dead brambles hook his trousers.

Cat Palmer says he feels bored and tired; Jeremy's so weak from the exertion of freeing himself that they both stop dead in their wet boots and can't get breath.

Land white as a bride, from the frozen lake to the pavements.

In houses across the park people have left their curtains open. Winking trees stand in most windows. Jeremy Potts says, What about knocking on a door and asking if we can borrow a child for the night? A kid with brown hair who would look at us the way kids look at their dads. We'd go to the mall and walk through the supermarket hand in hand. The mall has big glass doors, two sets. Inside everything is for sale.

Cat Palmer grins. He doesn't know what he's grinning at or why he feels so lost, though lost is what he feels. With a guide and all. A native to every neck of these woods. As if he no longer knows where he is, as if nothing is familiar, nothing belongs. Nothing attaches itself to him, nothing is his.

There is an old trailer parked on the empty lot at the seedy end of the park. Lights stream from the windows around the faces of children looking out, and it is not his home.

Remember Ellie? asks Cat. Remember Shirl's sister, JP?

Yeah, sure, says Jeremy.

Wasn't she nice?

Yeah, she was real nice, says Jeremy.

They drag on through the snow. In a moment, Cat thinks, unless he takes his thoughts in hand, he will recognize every single street, bent stop sign, footprint. He'll remember all the love he had for Ellie, all the love he's ever misplaced, and he will be lost in a worse way. He tells himself this: if he keeps walking, he'll get to the building in which he lives. He'll invite Jeremy inside to spend Christmas. He'll put the kettle on. Warm his and Jeremy's feet in hot water, their fingers round a bowl of tea. When he gets home he'll put on the kettle, get Shirl to come on over.

At last the children climb into their warmest clothes, Ellie Jones opens the door, and they all bustle through the thick snow to the stable where they find cows, chickens, sheep, goats, turkey soldiers strutting the shadows, and on the other side of the barn fathers waiting with sleighs and horses to take them home.

Now is the time for the youngest child to open the last door of the Advent calendar taped to the rough wood of a stall.

Lucy Heppellmeyer wades through the straw and has to be held high so she can reach. Kermit Jones and the fathers peer in through the back window. Everyone listens to the animals breathing, the impatient horses in the snow; everyone smells the warm manure, and feels drowsy.

Behind the last door is a city, a tiny shining city swirling with snow, and in a room in a tall brick building in the middle of the city two men and a woman crouch on the linoleum over an old-fashioned hip tub, filled to the brim. In a corner a broom planted upside down in a saucepan is decorated with feathers. Shirl Mortimer snaps the scissors in the air; she smiles at Cat, then at Jeremy. Cat Palmer carefully secures the struggling lobster so that its taped claws are accessible; and because the city is hundreds of miles from the nearest sea, Jeremy Potts is shaking salt into the deep water.